HOMECOMING HEART

HOMECOMING HEART

Mary Mackie

Chivers Press   •   Thorndike Press
Bath, England   Waterville, Maine USA

This Large Print edition is published by Chivers Press, England, and by Thorndike Press, USA.

Published in 2003 in the U.K. by arrangement with the author.

Published in 2003 in the U.S. by arrangement with Juliet Burton Literary Agency.

U.K. Hardcover ISBN 0–7540–8809–X (Chivers Large Print)
U.K. Softcover ISBN 0–7540–8810–3 (Camden Large Print)
U.S. Softcover ISBN 0–7862–4772–X (General Series Edition)

The text of this Large Print edition is unabridged.
Other aspects of the book may vary from the original edition.

Set in 16 pt. New Times Roman.

Printed in Great Britain on acid-free paper.

British Library Cataloguing in Publication Data available

Library of Congress Cataloging-in-Publication Data

Mackie, Mary.
    Homecoming heart / Mary Mackie.
      p.   cm.
    ISBN 0–7862–4772–X (lg. print : sc : alk. paper)
    1. Fathers—Death—Fiction. 2. Large type books. I. Title.
PR6063.A2454 H66 2003
                             2002028918

CHAPTER ONE

Drifting up from sleep, Jenny was first aware of a throbbing pain in her head. She could hear traffic not far away. The clump of heels down a corridor was accompanied by voices and laughter, and from closer yet came a regular bleeping sound that made her uneasy. The place smelled of what might have been soap. As she came nearer to full awareness, she recognised a constriction around her right arm as being caused by bandages. She was, she realised, in a hospital.

She opened her eyes, shocked by what her senses told her. Beside her bed, a machine was blipping in time with her heart-beats. She was connected to it by electrodes taped to her chest, and to a saline drip by a tube that snaked under the bandage on her arm. A tautness at her hairline was caused, as her fingertips discovered, by a plaster over a dressing. And she was wearing a shapeless cotton garment tied at the back. What was she doing here? What had happened?

A gust of recollection swept her back to full reality and she remembered her apartment in far away Hartford, Connecticut, USA, where she had been only yesterday. Was it only yesterday? The phone had rung and over a crackly transatlantic line Adam Carfield had told her the dreadful news that had left her unnaturally calm and controlled, able to function, but dead inside. In a state of shock, she had flown the Atlantic to London and, without sleep for thirty-six hours, had taken the morning train heading north, heading for Derbyshire and the home she had not seen for six long years.

The train crash had happened just south of Sheffield. Jenny remembered the confusion of screams, falling baggage, people tossed from their seats, and then darkness had claimed her. But evidently she had been lucky—she was still alive.

Alive . . . but alone. The thought fell numbly into the emptiness inside her as she tried to imagine a world which no longer contained her father.

Seeking escape from the grief that came crowding like a dark, suffocating mist, she struggled to raise herself and take note of unfamiliar surroundings. The room was pleasant enough, golden with evening sunlight that lit the tops of trees beyond the window. Modern prints hung against cream walls, a bedside cabinet had the usual drawer over a cupboard, there was a trolley, currently pushed aside, with a 'vital signs' chart hanging from its end, and in a vase on the low table between two chairs a dozen pink roses looked almost too perfect to be real.

Roses? From whom? But her head ached

too much to find an answer and she thrust the mystery aside as the squeak of soft shoes on rubber-tiled flooring announced the arrival of a nurse.

'Now, now, we're supposed to be resting,' the middle-aged woman crooned, hurrying to push Jenny down onto her back, at the same time consulting the dials and screens on the machine.

'But I feel fine!' Jenny protested.

'Do you, indeed?' The nurse pursed her lips, her brow furrowing as she studied her patient's pale face. Then she conceded, 'Well, let's see what the doctor has to say about that. You just lie still a bit longer until he comes.'

Jenny lay quietly, trying not to think about anything. It wasn't difficult with her head aching as though someone were stabbing a knife through her left eye and into her brain.

After a while the nurse returned with a sister and a cheerful young doctor who made examinations which assured him his patient was recovering. He gave permission for the machine to be disconnected, though the drip 'had better stay until the morning'. 'Right, then!' he concluded with a smile for Jenny. 'You can start to get back to normal. Like to sit up a bit? All right, Nurse, make her comfortable. Let her eat if she wants to. See you in the morning, Miss Hollander.'

The nurse came to help Jenny sit up while she adjusted the pillows, settling Jenny back against the cool nest created. A junior brought a bowl of warm water and Jenny submitted to having her hands and face gently washed and dried.

Folding her patient's slender hands against white linen, the nurse winked, tapped her nose and opened a drawer in the side table. She brought out something which she held up between finger and thumb. 'You'll want to be wearing this, I expect. We took it off in case you caught it and hurt yourself.'

Reaching for Jenny's left hand, she slipped the square-cut emerald ring onto the third finger, pausing a moment to admire it with open envy. 'It must have cost a fortune. You're a lucky girl. *My* old man couldn't afford a proper engagement ring. Still, we've been happy enough for eighteen years, which can't be bad. I'll just take your temperature. Open your mouth.'

Jenny did as she was told, glad of the thermometer as a barrier to speech. She felt too apathetic to correct the nurse's assumptions about the ring. Let it go for now; it didn't matter.

Having marked the chart, the nurse began to straighten the coverlet and tuck it firmly under the mattress. 'You can have some dinner in a few minutes,' the nurse chatted. 'That'll make you feel better. I expect your young man will be in again this evening. He'll be glad to see how much you've improved.'

4

'Young man?' Jenny queried, licking dry lips.

Eyebrows tilting, the nurse glanced at the ring sparking green on Jenny's hand. 'You mean to say you don't remember him? Maybe that bump on your head was more serious than we thought.'

'I only meant . . .' Jenny began, and sighed wearily, a hand to her throbbing head. 'No, nothing. It doesn't matter.'

Smiling a knowing smile, the nurse said, 'I didn't think you could have forgotten him. Maybe I should have said "your fiancé"—Mr Carfield. Adam Carfield, isn't it? What a nice young man. Lovely manners. Good-looking, too. It was him who arranged this private room—and him who brought these lovely roses for you. Very concerned, he seemed. Well, naturally enough, in the circumstances.'

Jenny wondered if the dismay that flowed through her showed in her face. Her cheeks felt to be burning as if with fever. But she could hardly explain that the nurse had written her own, completely fictional, scenario—one emerald ring, one young man, one love story: QED—except that it was built on circumstantial evidence and false assumption. It wasn't true.

'I'll bring you a jug of water,' the nurse said, giving a final tug to the coverlet. Then on an afterthought she reached into the bedside cabinet and brought out Jenny's capacious handbag. 'A dab of make-up wouldn't go amiss, if you feel up to it. You were still clutching your bag when they found you. It rode with you on the stretcher.'

'Thank you.' Jenny's fingers stroked familiar grey leather as if the bag were an old friend. It was intact with all her documents, her money and personal bits and pieces. What a relief! 'Do you know what became of my cases?'

'No, I'm sorry, I don't know anything about them. But don't worry, someone will be dealing with all that. You'll get them back. It was all a bit chaotic, you know. Three coaches derailed. Twenty-two people injured. But only one still in intensive care. It was a miracle. It could have been a lot worse.'

'Yes, indeed.' Jenny shivered as she thought of it. Yes, she had been lucky.

*   *   *

She managed to eat most of the meal which was brought to her; she was surprisingly hungry. The food restored some of her spirit and when she remembered that Adam Carfield might be coming she reached again for her handbag, extracting a make-up case and a hairbrush.

Her mirror told her how wan she looked. Eyes of a misty green stared back at her, shadowed with tiredness in a pallid face that was marked by a blue bruise along one cheek,

6

and by the plaster applied to her forehead. She used a dab of mascara, a touch of lipstick, but was too weak to do more than brush listlessly at her hair. It was thick and fair, brightened by sunlight, and she kept it short in a style that would toss into place, but it looked flat and lifeless.

Sighing, Jenny put her mirror away. Why should she worry about looking good, especially for Adam Carfield? There was no guarantee he would come, anyway.

The nurse had misunderstood the situation. Jenny wasn't engaged to anyone—especially not to Adam Carfield. Another man had given her the emerald, but it was not an engagement ring. At least . . . not officially. Not yet. She had been trying to make up her mind. But now, lying here in the hospital bed, the thought of having someone to care for her was suddenly very appealing.

Somewhere a clock was chiming seven. A shuffle of feet sounded along the corridor as visitors made for the main ward; then slower, firmer footsteps paused at her door and unconsciously she held her breath, watching the door swing open.

Adam Carfield made his taut face smile for her, though his eyes remained wary. 'Hello, Jenny. How are you feeling?'

Discovering her hands to be clutching the covers, she forced them to relax, and licked her dry lips. 'Not so bad. And you?'

'I'm fine.'

He didn't look fine; he looked tired. Otherwise, he had hardly changed in the six years since she had last seen him—years which had brought him to the age of thirty-two. He remained tall and sturdy, with dark hair parted off-centre and falling in soft locks either side of a face which tended to thinness, with an attractive bone-structure set off by eyes of clear grey. He was wearing a black tie and a dark suit that made him look even taller and leaner than she remembered. Had he lost weight?

The sight of him reminded her of too much. To stop the memories from overwhelming her she blurted: 'Adam, I know how busy you must be. I'm sorry to add extra problems.'

'It's hardly your fault,' he broke in. 'I'm sorry, too—for you. Things were bad enough for you without all this.'

'I'll survive.'

Again he forced a smile. 'Well, let's hope so. I've brought your cases. Shall I bring them in?'

Jenny was relieved to see her belongings. Adam was being awfully kind. Somehow she hadn't expected kindness from him.

'How did you manage to find them?' she asked.

'All the bags from the crash were being held at a central depot for collection. Fortunately yours were clearly labelled.'

'It was a kind thought.'

'The least I could do.'

They were being awfully stiff with each other, she thought. The situation must be as trying for him as it was for her, though he was affecting a brisk practicality to conceal his real feelings, whatever they were. Since she had no close relatives left, and since Adam had been closest to her father, fate had thrown her into his hands, at least until she was recovered from the effects of the accident. It was not what either of them could regard as a comfortable arrangement.

He said, 'You're looking pretty good, anyway. You must be tough, for all you look so delicate. I gather the doctor's pretty sure there's no real damage beyond cuts and bruises.'

'Yes, that's right. I was lucky.'

She wished he would relax. He stood there in his dark suit and black tie with his feet braced, as though he might make some excuse to leave at any minute.

He said: 'I want you to know that . . . that I share your sorrow. Your father was a good friend to me. More than a friend, he treated me like one of the family. I shall miss him very much.'

'Yes. Yes, I know.' Despite a hoarseness in her voice she was in control of herself. She felt she had accepted her father's death with admirable maturity, though as yet it didn't seem real to her. Right now nothing seemed

9

real.

'I meant to get changed before I came,' Adam said with a gesture at his dark suit, 'but there wasn't time. People hung around at the house longer than I expected. Of course your father was a popular man. The church was full.'

Jenny stared at him, shock turning her cold. 'The funeral?'

'It was this afternoon.' Seeing her turn paler than ever, he frowned in concern. 'You've been unconscious for over forty-eight hours. Didn't you realise?'

Forty-eight hours? she thought. Two whole days? 'No one told me. Oh, Adam . . . that's terrible. I should have been there!'

'It would only have been an ordeal for you. Everybody understood. Look . . . the sister told me you'll be discharged in a few days. You'll come to Yethfall House, of course.'

'Of course.' Why did he make it sound as if her destination was in doubt? Yethfall House was her home; she had been born there. Only the break-up of her parents' marriage had forced her to leave, but it had remained her father's home, where she had visited him.

With a cold shock she realised that her father would not be there, not ever again. It was inconceivable.

'I nearly came home last Christmas,' she croaked, twisting the edge of the sheet around her finger. 'I wish I had. It just wasn't very

10

convenient. But I could have made it, if I'd known . . .'

'You couldn't have known,' Adam said. 'Your father didn't mind. He knew you'd made a new life for yourself. Don't worry about it.'

'But I do worry! I should have come home sooner. I knew he wasn't getting any younger. I just thought there'd be more time!' She fought back tears, and a choking anger. How dare he assume the right to tell her what her father had thought and felt? It was Adam's fault that she hadn't been home for six years.

Knowing she was being unfair made the tears press harder behind her eyes and she flung up her hands to cover them.

'Cry if you want to,' Adam said. 'It'll probably do you good.'

Jenny tore her hands away and faced him with stormy green eyes. 'Don't tell me what's good for me!'

He said nothing. Apart from a tightening of his mouth his face was devoid of expression as he returned her glare with cool grey eyes.

Reaching to the pack of tissues the nurse had placed at her bedside, Jenny tore one free and blew her nose. She was out of sorts, emotionally and physically off-balance. This was not the way she had imagined meeting Adam and she was angry with him on account of it. Here in the hospital bed she was at a disadvantage, her face bruised, her hair a mess, her only garment a shapeless hospital

11

gown. She felt so horribly guilty about everything.

'Is that an engagement ring you're wearing?' Adam observed with studied unconcern. 'I didn't know you were engaged.'

'Oh . . .' She touched the ring, twisting it on her finger. Though she never remembered making a conscious decision to lie, her mouth formed words that said: 'There wasn't time to tell anyone. It only happened a few days ago.'

'I see. So who's the lucky man?'

'His name's Warren. Warren Oxenford.'

'Your boss?'

'Yes.'

His brow furrowed. 'I had the impression, from what your father said, that your boss was nearly his age.'

The damp tissue became a wad in her fist. 'Did you? How strange.' She was quite sure that Adam wouldn't respond in any positive way to the news that the man she claimed as her fiancé was nearly thirty years her senior.

'Anyway,' he went on, 'judging by what he said, your father liked him. I'm sure he would have been delighted for you. He used to worry about your being alone when he was gone. He would have been glad to know you'd found someone to look after you.'

Fury had been building in her. Now it exploded. 'Don't *do* that!' she raged at him. 'Don't talk to me as if I were a silly child. I don't need "looking after". And will you please stop explaining my own father to me. He was *my* father, not yours!'

'I'm aware of that.'

His rock-like calmness grated on her, but she hadn't the strength to argue further. Leaning back against her pillows, she brushed a weary hand through the air. 'Oh . . . go away, Adam. Just go away and leave me alone!'

He departed without noise or fuss, leaving the door swinging briefly behind him. As silence closed round her, Jenny laid an arm across her aching eyes. She was riven with a misery that clamped tight round her chest and would not let her cry properly. Adam still hated her, she was sure.

Well, the feeling was mutual. It was because of him that she had kept away these last precious years. Because of him she had missed her chance to see her beloved father before it was too late.

*   *   *

Jenny had been just nine years old when her parents split up and her mother took her to live in America, with a stepfather who remained around for three years until that marriage too ended in divorce. From the age of twelve Jenny had been raised by her mother alone—a woman left bitter and disillusioned by her experiences and determined not to let her daughter fall into the same trap.

On occasion Miriam Hollander Blake had wearied of maternal responsibility, and when these periods of ennui occurred Jenny had been shipped back to England to vacation with her father, who adored her. Her memories of those childhood holidays were all joyful.

She had often wished she could stay at Yethfall House being indulged and cossetted instead of returning to the condominium where her mother drank too much and stayed out all night with men-friends, but Jenny had felt she was needed there. Out of loyalty to her mother, she had kept the unpleasant truth from her father and filled her letters to him with news of her own doings, her progress at school and college, her hobbies and her friends.

In return, her father had written to her about his own life, which revolved around the family business—Hollander Craft Furnishings—a company which produced hand-made furniture for wealthy customers who appreciated, and could afford, the finest things. Henry Hollander was still main shareholder and managing director, as his father and grandfather had been before him. His only regret was that he had no son to carry on the tradition. He had often, jokingly, made reference to his dream that Jenny, his only child, might one day come back, join the family firm and take over when he retired.

As time passed, he had started to refer to

14

the talents of a new young business associate, Adam Carfield, whom he intended to train as his successor at Hollander Craft Furnishings. Jenny's mother, told about this, had poured vitriol—'The old fool's being taken for a ride. No young man's *that* much of a paragon. Write and tell your father he's an idiot to trust this Carfield. When you trust, you get burned. I should know. It happened twice to me.'

Jenny was fifteen when first she met Adam Carfield, who was eight years her senior. She liked him on sight, and for a while suffered the pangs of a teenage crush which, fortunately, faded when her life in the States reclaimed her.

And then, in the summer of her eighteenth year, Jenny had finished college and returned for another, longer holiday in the dales. Now that she was grown, a mutual attraction flared between her and Adam Carfield, and with her father's approval they went out on dates, playing tennis and dancing; they went swimming, and driving to dine at picturesque inns, coming home beneath skies bright with stars. Inevitably, the relationship had become more than platonic. But neither of them had let emotion run too hot and high. The embraces Jenny had shared so enthusiastically with Adam had been, for her, just part of the fun of that summer. She was not ready for commitment. She had thought that Adam understood that.

15

So she had been amazed and embarrassed when, on her last night in England, he had gone down on one knee and formally proposed marriage. She hadn't meant to laugh—that had been a result of pure nervous embarrassment. But Adam had taken it as an insult.

'I suppose you think you're too good for me,' he had said, eyes cold as ice in a face like stone. 'Well, have a good laugh, Jenny, and go back and tell about the poor idiot who believed your smiles and your kisses. You're just like all the rest of your generation—fickle and faithless. I bet you'd even have slept with me, if I hadn't been so careful to behave like a gentleman. Did that amuse you, too? Are the boys at college so bashful? How many of them have you bedded?'

The insult had inflamed Jenny. Already off-balance, she had been riven with a rage that made her lash out without thought, her hand connecting solidly with the side of Adam's face.

'Bitch!' he had flung at her through his teeth.

It was the last thing he had said to her.

That was the last time she had been home to England. Until now. She had made excuses, afraid of being obliged to meet Adam again, and somehow six years had slipped by. Six long years. How stupid it all was, and all because of Adam Carfield.

On her return to the States Jenny had plunged into a course in business studies which led her eventually to become PA to a wealthy businessman who conducted his various concerns from an office in Hartford, Connecticut. Warren Oxenford was old enough to be her father—in fact he had a son, Peter, who was a year or so older than she—and at first their relationship had been purely that of assistant and boss. But when her mother died very suddenly, in circumstances too painful even now to contemplate in detail, Warren had been a rock of support and comfort.

After that, Jenny had slowly realised that her employer cared for her in a personal way. He had revealed his feelings gradually, anxious not to crowd her but nonetheless determined to win her. He wasn't the sort to give up easily. Jenny had resisted, but she was loath to do anything that would irrevocably harm their relationship. She had grown fond of him and valued his friendship.

When her own father had come over for a visit—because she appeared to be too busy to visit *him* any more, he had observed—she had taken the chance to get him and Warren together, to see if they clicked. They did. They liked each other just fine; but the immediate rapport between them had made Jenny's dilemma more difficult. Were fondness, respect, and mutual loneliness a good enough

17

basis for marriage?

Marriage was what Warren had in mind. He alluded to it frequently, assuring her that her uncertainty did not alter his feelings for her. He understood her doubts. He was prepared to be patient. But he kept nibbling away at the barriers, inexorable as water dripping on stone. Last Christmas he had given her the emerald ring—not as an engagement token, not exactly, though his intentions had been clear enough: 'Wear it as a dress ring—for now. I'll not rush you, honey. Just wear it to remind you I'm here if you need me.'

Dear Warren, that was so like him—always anxious to do what was best for her, never pushy, ever patient and understanding. She loved him for it, of course she did, but that grateful sort of loving and being 'in love' were two different things. Did the difference matter? Wasn't a comfortable fondness maybe preferable to fireworks and stars?

Jenny looked at the ring, sitting on the third finger of her left hand where the nurse had mistakenly placed it. Why had she left it there? Why had she lied about it to Adam? What was she afraid of?

It had nothing to do with Adam! she told herself. It had been her own innermost instinct speaking, telling her what her conscious mind as yet refused to accept—that she loved Warren and wanted to be his wife. That was the truth of it. The age difference wasn't

18

important, nor the fact that Warren had been married before and had a grown son who rather resented Jenny. None of that mattered. She needed a refuge. She would find it in Warren's mature strength.

CHAPTER TWO

Adam did not come to visit her again, though the nurses said he kept check on her progress by phone. However, other friends of her father arrived to express their sympathy and concern, and her room was soon festooned with flowers and 'Get Well' cards.

A special visitor was Louise Glenford, who had been housekeeper to Henry Hollander for fifteen loyal years. She had always made Jenny feel welcome at Yethfall House. Now, however, there was mutual sorrow to bind them as Louise told Jenny of her father's collapse.

'I don't know how I'd have managed without Mr Carfield. He's been so kind. He just took over and made all the arrangements, though he was as upset as I was. He was very fond of your father, you know.'

'It was mutual between them, wasn't it?' Jenny said, the lump of her own grief sitting in her chest like a stone.

'Oh, yes, I'm sure it was. Your father always said that if he'd had a son he would have wanted him to be just like Mr Carfield.'

Instead, Jenny thought, Henry Hollander had had a daughter, who hadn't been around when she was finally needed—and all because of Adam Carfield. More and more she found herself resenting the way Adam appeared to have usurped her place in her father's affections.

'Have there been any calls for me?' she asked. 'From the States?'

'From your fiancé?' Louise said with a sad smile. 'No, I'm afraid not, love. Why, were you expecting him to call?'

'Just wondered. I, um . . . gather that Adam told you about . . .'

'He said you were engaged. I'm really happy for you, Jenny. You'll be glad of some support at a time like this. Couldn't he have come with you? Or will he follow on later?'

'I'm not sure. He couldn't get away at once. Business commitments, you know.'

How she hated lying. The sooner this whole tangle was straightened out, the better. She would have to talk to Warren and make this 'engagement' a reality.

Later that evening, she asked for the phone. The time difference meant that Warren ought to be in his office at OxenCo, but when she asked the receptionist to connect her with Mr Oxenford it was the voice of Peter, Warren's son, which said: 'Well, it's about time! Is this the first minute you've had to think about Dad?'

'I've thought about him constantly,' Jenny said stiffly. 'Things have been difficult here. Is he around? May I speak with him?'

'The boss is out today,' Peter said. 'You

21

want to leave a message?'

Jenny hesitated, wondering how he might distort anything she said. He was jealous of her relationship with his father and would make mischief if he could. 'Tell him I'm okay. And give him my love. I'll call again maybe tomorrow evening.'

'I'll pass the message. So when do we expect you back?'

'I'm not sure. I haven't yet had a chance to talk to the lawyers or anything, so . . .'

'Well, don't rush it. Nobody here is missing you. Your replacement PA is doing just fine.'

Subtle cruelty was part of his nature, but it still stung. 'I'm glad to hear it.'

'In fact,' he said, 'it might be best if you decide to stay over there. People are starting to talk.'

'About what?'

'About you and my dad. The grapevine's really humming. What else did you expect when it's known that the boss is tumbling his personal assistant?'

For a moment Jenny was too horrified to reply, then she said flatly, 'That's not true, Peter, and you know it. Your father and I are very close, but—'

'Oh, sure. Just good friends. But that's not what people are saying. It's about time you realised what's going on here. My father's being made to look a fool because of you. The best thing would be for you to resign right

22

away. If you've got to continue this tacky relationship, at least keep it out of the office.'

Jenny was silent, sickened to know that she and Warren had become the subject of malicious gossip. Their relationship was one of mutual comfort, no more than platonic so far, but vicious minds had obviously read much more into it.

'Does he know about the gossip?' she asked.

'I've made sure he does, but he's been reluctant to tell you. If he told the truth, he'd agree with me—you'd do better to quit OxenCo and go right away.'

'I don't believe that,' Jenny said, her voice low and tremulous. 'That's you talking, not Warren. There's another way to stop the gossip, Peter. I can marry your father.'

'That's what you're angling for, isn't it?' came the sneering reply. 'But even you have to wait to be asked—or are you so liberated you'll propose to *him*?'

'If you must know, he's asked me several times already. He's the one who's waiting.'

The line sang in the moment before he said bitterly, 'I've known all along you were baiting hooks. He's a rich man, and he's lonely, a ripe catch. Well, try it. But you'll have to go through me to do it. I'll die before I let any scheming little fortune-hunter call herself my stepmother.'

The phone went dead and after a moment Jenny let the receiver drop back into the cradle as though it were a dead rat. She had always known that Peter disliked her, but until now he had been subtle in his opposition. Which one would Warren side with—his only son, or the young woman he professed to love?

*   *   *

Adam Carfield owned a silver-blue Ford Granada, powerful and elegant, and he drove the way he did most things, with calm efficiency. Sitting beside him, Jenny watched the suburbs of Sheffield dwindle into the Derbyshire countryside, hills and valleys with woods wearing several shades of fresh green in the May sunlight. Pink and white blossom bloomed, with lilac adding its own glory. She was reminded of Connecticut and couldn't decide whether the ache she felt was for her adopted home or her native land. All her life she had been torn—between her father and her mother, between England and the States.

Now she was aware of yet another rift— between her affection for Warren Oxenford, and her more mixed emotions concerning the dark, quiet man beside her. She had always found him attractive, but now he made her feel defensive and guilty. She resented the way he appeared to have taken over, but she was grateful to him for his concern and interest. He was doing it for her father's sake, of course. How he felt about Jenny herself, under that very British self-control, it was impossible to guess.

Glancing at her for the tenth time as she sat relaxed in the comfortable seat, Adam said yet again, 'Okay?'

'I keep telling you, I'm fine. All I had was a few cuts and bruises.'

'And a bump on your head, which kept you out cold for two days.'

'They wouldn't have let me leave hospital if I hadn't been okay. Stop worrying about me. I'm not your responsibility.'

His look said he could argue about that if he wanted. 'I gather you made some phone calls,' he said, watching the road. 'Did you talk to your fiancé?'

'I tried. I couldn't reach him.'

'Maybe he's on a flight to your side.'

'He's not.'

'How can you be so sure? You left a message, didn't you? If I were in his shoes, I'd want to make sure that you were all right.'

'I . . . didn't say anything about the accident,' Jenny admitted, staring out of the side window away from him. 'There was no point in worrying him. It's not as if I'm badly hurt. It would have been a waste of time for him to come all this way, especially when he's busy. He's trying to finalise a deal before his competitors get there.'

'What business is he in?'

'Electronics. Computers and software

mainly. But he diversifies.'

'And he's wealthy, naturally. Emeralds like that don't come out of cut-price jewellers'.'

Detecting a hint of derision in his tone, she said: 'He's a fine man. When Mother died, he was wonderful. He kept me from going completely to pieces. I love him very much. I'd love him if he didn't have a bean.'

Adam slanted her a look from expressionless eyes. 'You don't have to convince me, Jenny. It's your life.'

She twisted her head away from him again, wincing as a pain shot up her neck. Just being with Adam made her feel irritable. She wanted to scream at him for being so calm when all her nerves were on edge. She couldn't bear to be around him much longer.

Her head had started to pound by the time the car reached the familiar road into Yethfall village, cottages mostly painted white, around a church and a small shop and café. On a car-park, several vehicles had been left by tourists coming to walk the dale.

The Granada nosed steeply down a narrow hairpin lane into Yethfall Dale, heading ever downward beneath overhanging trees until it reached the bottom of the narrow valley. The road ended at a stream beyond which the tree-clad hillside rose almost vertically, dappled green and achingly familiar.

Adam pulled in by the high wall of Yethfall House before getting out to open the gates.

Jenny watched him dully, admiring the lean lines of his body and his economy of movement. Today he was dressed in grey slacks with a blue shirt and a black tie. The jacket to his suit was slung over the back seat of the car.

What was he really thinking? she wondered. What was he feeling? Since they first met at the hospital he had effectively shut her out, leaving her no idea whether he still remembered the way she had treated him six years before. She had been very young—only eighteen, and just a little spoiled and silly. She hadn't intended to hurt him. Surely he understood that?

Returning to the car, he drove slowly between the gates. Now Jenny could see the white house sprawling below the wooded hill, behind stone steps, with lawns and flower-beds laid out in front of it, all secluded from the dale by a tall brick wall. At the far end of the garden, trellises draped in greenery hid the vegetable plot, while central to one of the lawns a stone mermaid dreamed over a pool which would soon be thick with lilies.

Home, Jenny thought, and with pain remembered that her father would not be there to greet her.

'I'll just drop you off and see you safely with Louise,' Adam said, 'then I must get back to the office.'

'That's fine. Don't worry about me. Now

27

I'm home I'll be okay. And . . . thank you, Adam. It was good of you to bring me.'

As the car rolled up to stop by the steps, Jenny glimpsed old Tom Hackenthwaite, the gardener, peering from behind the trellis to see her arrive. Then a movement by the door diverted her attention as Louise appeared, and a red setter came hurtling out of the house.

'That's Gem,' Adam said as he climbed from the car. 'He's fussy, but he won't hurt you. You don't mind dogs, do you?'

'No, not at all.'

The dog bounded round Adam in a passion of pleasure, then came to afford the same affections to Jenny, who bent to pet him, then raised her voice to say: 'You didn't tell me we'd acquired a dog, Louise.'

'He's not Louise's, he's mine,' Adam said, slamming the boot after removing her cases.

Puzzled, Jenny lifted an arm to guard her aching eyes from the sun as she squinted at him. 'Yours? Then what's he doing here?'

Adam hesitated, then said, 'He lives here. And so do I. I thought you knew that.'

'You *live* here?' She was so startled she could hardly think. 'Since when?'

'Since about a year ago. Your father needed the company.'

Was that another subtle criticism? she wondered. 'I see. No—I don't see. You had the flat over the offices. Why did you move?'

'We needed the flat for the new accounts

28

manager. It was convenient all round for me to move here.'

'But what will you do now?'

He shrugged. 'Stay here, I suppose. I like the old place, and if you're getting married you won't want it.'

Jenny struggled with a feeling of unreality. 'No, I guess not.'

'We'll talk about it later,' he suggested. 'I must get back to work. Have to keep Hollander's ticking over, for both our sakes. You're my partner now, you know. I'll see you at dinner.'

Lying on her bed, Jenny stared at a ceiling tinted rose by the glow through pink linen curtains. Adam lived here, at Yethfall House? Why had no one told her? She had not anticipated being plunged so intimately into his company. Nor had she really thought what her father's death would mean. Since she had been Henry Hollander's only close relative, presumably his estate would come to her—the house, and the business.

Peter Oxenford could hardly accuse her of fortune-hunting, not if she became financially independent; but the inheritance could change her life in many ways. She might finally fulfil her father's dream—she might decide to take on the job of managing Hollander Craft Furnishings.

The workers at Hollander's were craftsmen, using only the best woods and fabrics. Pieces from stately homes all over Britain, and from abroad, came to the riverside workshops to be refurbished with loving care. Jenny had seen something of this work during her summer vacations, when her father would proudly show her round his workshops and introduce her to his employees. He had often said how he would love to have her work with him some day, and in the back of her mind she had wondered if this might be possible despite opposition from her mother. Then the problem with Adam had intervened and she had settled for working at OxenCo, with Warren.

Now, suddenly, she was a senior partner in Hollander Craft Furnishings. But how could she stay in England when she was planning to marry Warren Oxenford? Nor, probably, would it be easy for her to work alongside Adam Carfield. The whole thing was fraught with too many problems. But what was her alternative—to sell up everything her father had loved and worked for, to leave Adam Carfield in charge?

'Oh, damn Adam Carfield!' she said aloud. Everywhere she turned, he was in the way.

Her father had kept secrets, now she came to think of it. Never once had he mentioned having Adam live with him. It seemed very odd.

Trying to relax, she let her glance stray round the room. Her father had had it redecorated recently, perhaps in the hope that she might soon visit. The wallpaper was strewn with swirls of pink rosebuds, charming but a little old-fashioned for her taste, and the bedcovers had been replaced by a duvet in toning pink. It hurt her to imagine the care her father must have taken in choosing the colour scheme, trying to please her, looking forward to seeing her. Now she was here, and it was too late.

Sleep drifted over her unexpectedly and she woke to see Louise coming in with a tray.

'I thought you'd be ready for a cup of tea,' the housekeeper said with a smile. 'Have you had a nap? You'll have to take it easy for a few days. Don't go overdoing things.'

'I've a feeling you won't let me do that,' Jenny said, pushing herself up on one elbow. 'Dear Louise, what would we do without you?'

'I'm very happy here. It's my home. I'd hate to leave it.'

'You won't have to. You can stay here and look after it for me. I'll be coming back often, even after I'm Mrs Warren Oxenford.' She gazed around the room, imagining showing the house to Warren. 'He'll love it. It's so English.'

When she looked back at Louise she saw that all colour had drained from the housekeeper's face and her jaw had dropped so that she was almost gaping.

'Why, what's wrong?' Jenny asked.

Louise collected herself, smiled a smile that

lasted half a second, and said, 'Nothing. It was just hearing you talk about being married. It sounded strange. You have your tea. And don't come down until you feel really rested. We'll have dinner at seven, as usual.'

When she had gone, Jenny stared at the closed door, wondering why Louise had lied to her. There was something going on that no one was prepared to talk about as yet. Adam, too, had seemed evasive and anxious to escape.

Feeling rested, she took a shower and washed her hair, drying it into its usual glossy shape, swept back from her face with a soft wing above her eyes. The bruises on her cheek and the contusion on her forehead were fading now, but she applied a light make-up to cover the traces. Having finished the chore, she turned swiftly away, hating to face eyes which stared back heavy with sadness. Her father had always disapproved of mourning, calling it self-indulgent. He would prefer her to get right on with her life.

She put on a skirt and top in silk jersey, a pale silver green which Warren said complemented her eyes. He liked her to wear green. That was why he had chosen an emerald for her ring.

She glanced at the ring, which she had again put on her left hand. It wasn't a pretence, it was only a little presumptuous of her when she had had no chance to tell Warren she was ready to marry him. The ring seemed like a talisman to protect her, though why she should feel in need of protection she did not know. What was she afraid of? Adam Carfield? What nonsense!

It was strange going down to dinner and finding Adam waiting for her in the big sitting-room where it had been her father's habit to relax. The setter, Gem, was there, too, friendly as ever until Adam told him to 'Sit!' after which the dog lay down on the hearth rug and seemed to go to sleep.

As though he belonged there and she was the visitor, Adam offered her a drink and invited her to sit down. She watched him by the drinks cabinet, thinking that six years had matured him, added confidence and an undoubted presence. He was not a man to be ignored. Was he a man to be watched?

He glanced round and caught her eyes on him. 'Ice?'

'Thank you.'

For a moment he stared at her as if trying to read her mind, but Jenny too could hide her feelings if she wished. She gave him a polite smile and glanced away to study the familiar room.

Little had changed. Like all rooms in the house, the sitting-room was spacious and high-ceilinged. Long floral drapes hung at french windows which opened onto the terrace. The furniture was upholstered in floral cambric—

Hollander furniture, of course, made of finest matured beech and oak.

A log fire in the hearth took the slight chill off the spring evening, and flowers were softly arranged in vases. In a glass-fronted cabinet against the wall was displayed Henry Hollander's collection of pigs—made of porcelain, brass, wood or plastic, some jokey, some minutely lifelike. Jenny had always loved searching for another pig to add to the collection, so she was saddened to realise that that was yet another thing she would never again do for her father.

His presence remained almost tangibly in the room, his books orderly on their shelves, tidy piles of his magazines on fishing and stamp-collecting, and a copy of the latest newsletter from the Rolls Royce Owners' Club to which he had belonged. But here and there were touches foreign to her: a newspaper her father would never have read, and a chess set of white jade standing on a table in the corner. Her father had never liked games. The newspaper and the chess set were signs of Adam's occupancy.

Adam brought her a gin and tonic clinking with ice and she thanked him without looking at him. He sank down in a chair not far away, lifting his glass. 'Absent friends.'

The toast made her scalp feel tight but she fought against showing distress. 'Yes.'

'So how are you feeling now? Better for a

rest?'

'Much better.'

'You must take things easy for a while. Your system's had quite a shock. Your millionaire will allow you a week or so, I hope?'

'He told me to take all the time I needed.'

'Kind of him.'

For the first time since sitting down, she looked fully at him. 'He is kind!'

'That's what I said. Look, Jenny, do you have to keep going on the defensive? I know you're under strain, but so am I. Let's try to keep calm, shall we?'

'I'm perfectly calm.'

'Oh, yes. Calm as an aspen in a wind storm.' He held up a hand to stop her protests. 'All right, I'm sorry. We're both edgy. Hardly surprising, I suppose. You were saying—about your fiancé . . .'

'What about him?'

Adam regarded her with exasperation. 'I can't remember.' He stood up, sweeping a hand through his hair. 'Where's Louise got to? Dinner must be ready by now.'

A sizzling silence filled the room. Into it, she said, 'Adam, what was the real reason you moved in here?'

He swung round, frowning. 'I told you—we hired a new accountant who came at short notice and as his wife wasn't keen on being left behind the simplest answer was for them to have the flat and for me to come here.'

'Whose idea was that?'

'Your father's. Well, this house is huge for a man on his own. He was tired of his own company in the evenings.'

'He had Louise,' Jenny objected.

'That's not quite the same. She has her own rooms and keeps to them when she's not busy. But if my presence bothers you I'll move out while you're here.'

'I never said it bothered me.'

'No, but you were thinking it. If you prefer, I'll go.'

'Don't be ridiculous. There's plenty of room for both of us. We're both sensible adult people.'

There was no discernible expression on Adam's face as he said heavily, 'Yes, so we are,' but all at once the intimacy of their situation lay exposed, fraught with electric undercurrents. Memories rose like ghosts unbidden, of sunlit days filled with laughter and shared delight which had gone sour at the last.

'Anyway,' Jenny said with a nervous flick of her head, 'it won't be for long.'

'Even if it's only a few days, that's long enough for your fiancé to object, I would have thought.'

'Why should it worry him? He trusts me.'

A tilt of his eyebrow said he was sceptical about that. 'If I were him I wouldn't want my lady staying with some other man.'

36

'You mean he should worry about *your* integrity?' she asked with a scorn intended to conceal her twitching nerves.

A twisted smile was his reaction to that slander. 'I only mean it would take a saint not to be a bit jealous, in the circumstances.'

'What circumstances? Warren doesn't know you're living here, and even if he did I've never told him about—' She bit the words off, wishing she had not raised those particular ghosts.

But Adam said calmly, 'About what happened six years ago, you mean? If that's what's troubling you, Jenny, forget it. I have.'

He turned away as Louise came in to say that dinner was ready, which prevented him from seeing Jenny's face. She felt as though she had been slapped.

In the dining-room, Louise served home-made crab bisque followed by lamb steaks in redcurrant sauce. She had always been a superb cook but that evening she had taken extra trouble, even remembering Jenny's fondness for lemon soufflé, light and tartly sweet.

'Your memory is amazing,' Jenny remarked.

'It was one of your father's favourites, too,' Louise replied. 'He always had it on your birthday, to remind him of you.'

Realising afresh how lonely her father must have been, Jenny stared at her plate, and as Louise left the room, Adam said, 'Your father loved you very much, in case you didn't know.'

'I do know!' She glared at him with tear-bright eyes. 'I don't need you to tell me anything about him.'

Adam lifted an eyebrow in silent comment, then shrugged and said, 'Pardon me for breathing.'

'Just what's been going on here?' she demanded. 'Seems like you've taken over. You act as though you were one of the family, not just—'

'Not just what?' Adam asked in a low voice edged with anger, his face suddenly set in hard lines beneath its soft wings of dark hair, his grey eyes cold. 'Not just an employee? That always did stick in your craw. I was the hired help and you were the boss's daughter.'

'That's not true!'

'No, I don't suppose you ever admitted it to yourself. You were never one to recognise your own faults, any more than you really cared about the sort of life your father had here, all on his own these last few years, getting older all the time, with precious little to look forward to.'

'It wasn't my fault! And I did see Dad. He came over to the States that time. Besides . . . You must know why I didn't want to come. And anyhow it's none of your business!'

'You think not? I don't expect you to understand it, but your father and I became firm friends over the years and I cared about him. His well-being *was* my business. He was always good to me. If it's of the slightest interest to you, I never knew my own father.'

'So you latched on to mine!'

'Well, you didn't show any signs of wanting him!'

Unable to stand being in the same room with him any more, Jenny leapt from her chair and ran for the door. Adam moved faster, but as he reached for her she lashed out, only to have him capture her wrists in hard fingers, his eyes blazing down at her with cold grey fire.

'No woman slaps me twice!' he grated.

Drawing a deep, painful breath, she tipped back her head and looked him straight in the eye, cold and haughty. 'Please let me go. I don't like being manhandled.'

'That,' he returned, 'is not what you said six years ago.'

Her face burned and her head felt as though it might burst as she recalled the many summer nights when she had ended up in his arms, holding him as tightly as he held her, returning his kisses with passion and pleasure. How dare he remind her of it?

'I hate you!' she informed him with all the venom in her soul. 'I hate you!'

CHAPTER THREE

Later, when the house was quiet and in darkness, Jenny crept down to her father's study and used the phone to dial a transatlantic call to Warren's home. It seemed to ring for ages before someone answered.

'Hello? Warren?'

' 'Fraid not,' came a familiar voice. 'This is your friendly answering machine with the news that Mr Warren Oxenford is away on business. If you have a message, speak after the tone . . . Beep!'

Hearing female laughter in the background, Jenny turned cold,

'Stop fooling, Peter. I need to talk to your father. If he's not there, will you ask him to call me as soon as possible?'

'What's your number, please?' Peter was still playing for laughs and getting them from whichever girl he had in tow.

'He knows my number!'

'Then why hasn't he used it? Maybe he doesn't want to talk to you. Ever thought of that?'

She had thought of it, and dismissed it as unthinkable. 'Perhaps he's lost it. Is he really away?'

'Gone to the Big Apple. More conferences. Or maybe he's on the run from female predators.'

The background laughter made Jenny's skin crawl. 'What hotel is he staying at?'

'I've no idea.'

'Well, thanks for nothing, Peter,' Jenny said bitterly. 'Go back to your booze. But I'll keep calling until I get through to Warren.'

'Do that,' he replied, just audible as she slammed the phone down and put her hands to a head that felt to be bursting. Was Peter just playing games, or was Warren really avoiding her?

Going back to her room, she took two aspirins and fell into a shallow sleep filled with disturbing dreams from which she half-woke only to drift back into that nightmare world. She dreamed about the train crash, and her father—or was it Warren?—who appeared to be in some terrible danger. Her frantic efforts to save him were impeded by someone who held her back.

She came suddenly awake to find herself struggling with a man who was trying to calm her. 'Dad?' she breathed, still half in the dream.

'It's me—Adam. Wake up, Jenny.'

Shocked back to reality she lay still, gasping for breath, feeling tears cool on her face. The terror of her dream remained with her and now it was joined by real grief. Turning away from Adam she buried her face in the pillow, sobbing bitterly.

At first Adam tried to console her, pleading, 'Don't, Jen. It was a dream, that's all.' Then realising that more than nightmares had caused her distress he contented himself with stroking her hair and her shoulders. 'That's right. Cry. Cry it all out, Jenny Wren.'

'Don't call me that!' she managed, and whirled to face him with the sheet clutched over her thin nightdress. 'Only my father ever called me that!'

A moment's silence. In the dawn light she couldn't see his face clearly but she heard the pain in his voice as he said, 'I'm sorry. I only meant—'

Jenny lay down again, her back to him, silent tears streaming down her temple. Her thoughts were incoherent: she wanted her father, she wanted Warren, but it was Adam who was offering comfort and somehow that only increased her pain. If she had any pride, she would send him away, but she couldn't; she needed someone to be there. She needed not to be alone.

'Forgive me for the things I said last night,' Adam said. 'I loved your father, too. I've been raging inside. I suppose I wanted to lash out at someone and you got in the way. I'm sorry, Jen.'

'I wasn't very kind to you, either,' she whispered hoarsely.

'We're both under a strain.'

'Yes.'

'You okay now? Think you can sleep?'

'I think so.'

'Then I'll go.'

The bed gave as he got up from it and there was a pause, as if he were waiting there, perhaps considering saying more. Then she heard the soft click as the door closed behind him.

Jenny lay quite still, her eyes stinging. Kindness, from Adam, was almost more than she could bear.

She woke to the sound of a church bell calling people to morning service at the church on the hill. Later, emerging from the bathroom wrapped in towels, she found Louise Glenford bringing her breakfast.

'I heard water running,' the housekeeper smiled. 'Mr Carfield had breakfast ages ago, so I thought you might like to eat in your room and take your time.'

'You spoil me, Louise,' Jenny said. 'Thank you. Where's Adam now?'

'He took Gem for a run down the dale. I expect he'll be back soon, to get changed. He's going out to lunch. Perhaps you'd like to have yours in the garden. It's a lovely day.'

'That sounds like a good idea. So where's Adam going?'

Louise was throwing the curtains open to let sunlight in. 'He didn't say. But I think he has a date.'

'With whom?'

Louise shook the curtain straight and turned with a laugh. 'He didn't tell me that, either, though he's been seeing a lot of Cathy Brent lately. Do you remember her? Her father's the vicar of Saint Margaret's, in Shadwell.'

A vicar's daughter? Jenny thought with a twinge of disapproval. 'No, I don't think I ever met her.'

'Come to think of it, they only moved to this area a couple of years ago. I keep forgetting how long it is since you were here.'

'It wasn't entirely through choice,' Jenny said. 'I had other commitments. Mother, and my studies, my work . . .'

'I wasn't criticising,' Louise broke in.

Unnerved by the housekeeper's worried stare, Jenny let her gaze flicker away. 'I'm sorry. It's my own conscience keeps pricking me. I should have come before now. But at the time it seemed I had good reasons for putting it off, and putting it off.'

'Procrastination is the thief of time,' Louise quoted with a sad smile. 'That's what your father always used to say. But he understood. He never blamed you.' Her mouth was trembling and there was a hint of moisture in her eyes. 'He was a wonderful man, Jenny.'

'I know,' Jenny said hoarsely. 'We shall both miss him.'

A tear spilled down Louise's cheek. She said, 'Yes, we shall,' and rushed away as if to hide her distress.

Poor Louise, Jenny thought. She was an attractive woman, now in her later fifties, trim and well-groomed with little grey in her dark hair. She had never, to Jenny's knowledge, addressed her employer as anything other than 'Sir', or 'Mr Hollander', but evidently she had been fond of him. Poor Louise.

Sitting on the window-seat to eat her breakfast, Jenny sipped coffee and gazed along the lovely valley which stretched beyond the garden wall, her thoughts on Louise, and on Adam. He had a lunch date, with a girl named Cathy Brent. Why should that come as such a surprise? He was thirty-two years old, a normal, single, virile male.

She caught sight of a figure in the distance striding over humps and hollows of land beside the stream. A red setter bounded ahead of him, pausing to pick up a stick and race back with it, to have it thrown again. Seeing the pair coming this way made Jenny drink her coffee in gulps before throwing on a pair of jeans and a shirt.

By the time Adam came through the small gate beyond the trellis, Jenny was on the terrace, idly swinging a leg as she perched on the stone balustrade. Gem arrived first, hurling himself at her. Laughing, she petted him, fending off his attempts to lick her face as Adam started up the steps, dressed all in lean black that morning, jeans and shirt with the sleeves back to show the steel watch on his wrist.

'Well, good morning,' she greeted. 'What a lovely day.'

'Certainly is,' he said, stopping two steps below her. 'You look much better. How do you feel?'

'Fine.' Sudden self-consciousness made her bend to fuss the dog, an excuse to avoid Adam's eyes. 'I'm sorry I disturbed you in the night.'

'It was practically morning.'

'Even so . . .'

The ensuing silence sang in her ears until she was forced to look up. Now it was Adam's turn to slide his glance away.

'Don't give it another thought,' he said. 'Gem! Calm yourself down. You've had enough excitement for one morning.' Then he put on a smile that didn't reach his eyes. 'Well, I must get on,' he said, striding up the final two steps.

'I hear you have a date for lunch,' Jenny remarked.

He stopped, flicking her an unreadable look. 'That's right. I was going to ask you if you'd keep an eye on Gem for me.'

'Why? Is Cathy Brent allergic to dogs?'

'The grapevine's been busy, I see,' he commented dryly. 'As a matter of fact Cathy and Gem get along like a house on fire, but I'd sooner leave him here today. So—will you dog-sit for me?'

Jenny shrugged. 'I guess. What time will you be back?'

'I don't know. Why?'

'Because it's time we had a talk—a business talk. I need to know about Hollander's. And don't I have to see Dad's lawyers? There must be things to settle, papers to sign.'

His expression was guarded. 'Yes, that's true. I've arranged for the solicitor to come here tomorrow evening.'

'Tomorrow?'

'Even James Wickham doesn't like to work on Sundays. Besides, another day's rest will do you good. Settling a will is never a pleasant business.'

'Okay. Whatever you say.'

She watched him go inside the house, watched the door close behind him and Gem. Let him go off on his date. What did she care?

She spent most of the day wandering aimlessly round the house and garden with Gem at her heels. The dog was company, if nothing else, and he helped to distract her when sorrow lay heavy on her because of the gap left by her father's absence.

She tried again to phone Warren, only to be told by Maria his maid that he really was in New York and had not left the name of his hotel. Perhaps Peter would know.

'Yes, maybe so,' Jenny said dully, knowing that Peter would not give her any information.

'But if he calls, Maria, will you ask him to phone me? Take another note of my number here, will you?'

The day seemed endless. She lunched alone and dined alone. Where had Adam taken Cathy Brent? Jenny remembered a pleasant pub by a river, and a hotel on a hill, from where lovely walks could be taken. She and Adam had gone there several times during that summer when the world had been bright and innocent. He had been an amusing, attentive companion. Did Cathy Brent find him so?

What was she like, this vicar's daughter? Did she laugh at Adam's jokes? Did she walk hand in hand with him, her head brushing his shoulder as he drew her attention to a moorhen in the shadow of alders, or the play of sunlight on a hill? Did he stop occasionally with that special look in his eyes as he laid an arm about her shoulders and bent to kiss her?

Startled by her physical response to the vivid memories, Jenny shook herself and went to the french windows to look up at a sky where stars were brightening. She really didn't care what Adam was doing with Cathy. She wished she could stop thinking about it. If only Warren would call!

Eventually she went to bed, but she lay wakeful until she heard the Granada purr in through the gates, and then the grating slam of garage doors. Her window was open, so she heard Adam stride swiftly up the steps to

48

unlock the front door, and when he came along the upper hall he was whistling tunefully. Clearly he had enjoyed his day.

She overslept, so by the time she surfaced Adam had gone to the office. The remains of his breakfast still lay on the morning room table, and Louise was not in the house.

Jenny found Gem stretched on the terrace in the sunlight. He bounded up and came to lick her hand, red flanks quivering with pleasure. Having greeted him and stroked his soft ears, Jenny saw Louise along the garden cutting flowers and set out towards her.

'Well, good morning,' Louise greeted. 'Did you sleep all right? I'd have woken you earlier, but Mr Carfield said to let you rest.'

'He's giving the orders around here now, is he?' Seeing Louise blink, she added, 'He ought to have known I'd want to go in to Hollander's. I could have gone with him.'

'Oh, I . . . I don't suppose he expected you to be ready for that, not yet. You ought to rest a few days more.'

'I want to be doing something. Hanging around here only makes me depressed. Is Dad's car in the garage?'

Louise looked worried. 'You're surely not thinking of driving?'

'Why not?'

'Well, because . . . because it might not be wise. Besides, that car hasn't been on the road for a while. Lately, if your father wanted to go

49

anywhere, he let Mr Carfield drive him.'

'Did he? Why, wasn't he well? Louise, I thought—'

A voice from the vegetable garden made them both look round to see old Tom Hackenthwaite leaning on his hoe behind the budding clematis which draped the trellis. 'Begging your pardon, Miss Glenford,' he put in, cuffing sweat from his brow with a spotted handkerchief, 'but that there car's in tip-top condition. Mr Carfield had it taken for a thorough overhaul not two weeks ago, and I gave it a good clean only yesterday, thinking Miss Jenny might need it. It's got a full tank of petrol, Miss Jenny.'

'Thanks, Tom,' Jenny said gratefully, relieved to find an ally. 'So where will I find the keys?'

'On the keyboard by the back door,' he told her.

'I still don't think . . .' Louise began as Jenny moved away, but Jenny ignored her. It was such a relief to be doing something,

To her surprise, the car which remained in the double garage was not the stately vintage Rolls which had been her father's pride and joy, but a more modest saloon. Presumably her father had decided to sell the gas-guzzling Rolls and economise, and certainly the sporty VW Scirocco was more to Jenny's taste, but she was surprised no one had thought to tell her of the change.

The red car took the steep lane with ease and then she was out on the heights, passing by fields where sheep grazed among drystone walls and cloud-shadow undulated over hills and deep, hidden dales. Eventually she drove down into a broader valley where the town of Shadwell spread its grey houses and its riverside parks.

On the outskirts of the town, by the river where ducks and trout swam, lay the premises of Hollander Craft Furnishings. White fencing marked the perimeter, and the gate was flanked by boards painted with the name of the firm. A driveway led to low-profile buildings which held workshops and storerooms, with a main block containing showrooms on the ground floor, offices above, and on the top floor the flat where Adam had lived before he moved to Yethfall House.

Pulling in to a space in the staff car-park, Jenny made for the covered walkway which connected the main block with the workshops. In the fabric department, in a glass-walled office, the supervisor, Doris Brown, sat poring over a set of fabric swatches. Jenny tapped on the door and walked in, causing Doris to look up, her plain face registering displeasure.

'Yes?'

'Have I changed so much?' Jenny asked.

For a moment, Doris stared at her, then, 'Jenny! Oh, it's . . .' She stopped herself, coming out of her chair. 'I was going to say that it was lovely to see you, but in the circumstances . . . I can't tell you how sorry I am. The place won't be the same without your father.'

Doris had long been one of the stalwarts at Hollander's and she spoke from a sincere regard for her late employer. She was a dumpy woman who dressed for comfort rather than elegance, and for as long as Jenny could remember she had worn her hair in that pudding-cut bob with a brown hair-slide at one side. Now her hair was greying and the eyes magnified behind thick glasses had a faded look. Doris must be coming up to retirement age.

'Thank you, Doris. And how are you? Busy?'

'Busier than ever. We weren't too happy about some of the changes at first—a new broom, and all that—but Mr Carfield's policies are paying off.'

Mr Carfield's policies? Jenny thought, but her attention was distracted by the swatches of material lying on the desk—floral tapestry patterns in a variety of colours. 'What are these for?'

'A love-seat, would you believe?' Doris relaxed as the subject changed. 'For Lady Granton—at least I should say the Dowager Lady Frances, since her husband died. She has this beautiful old love-seat—but she also has about a dozen cats which she allows on her

52

furniture, so you can imagine. She wanted the love-seat restored, but the upholstery's beyond it. The piece will have to be re-covered, so I'm getting some samples ready to show her. Someone will go out to Granton Towers. Personal service has always been one of our boasts.'

'Yes,' Jenny smiled. 'I remember.'

Doris peered at her in concern. 'You look tired, my dear. Still getting over that accident, I suppose. You must take it easy.'

'You're supposed to tell me I look fine, to help my morale.'

'Well, you do, apart from being a bit pale. Still, you never were the rosy type. Pale and interesting, isn't that it?'

'So they tell me.'

The door flung open and suddenly Adam was there, trying to conceal his irritation, and his haste. 'Well Jenny! This is a surprise. What are you doing here?'

Jenny had the feeling he had been warned of her unexpected arrival and, disturbed by it, had rushed to find her. But that couldn't be right. Could it? 'I thought I'd come over and see Doris,' she said.

'You should have come up to the office first. Oh, Doris, I came to tell you Lady Frances called. She's going away for a few days, so unless someone can get over there today the samples will have to wait until next week. See what you can arrange, will you?' He turned back to Jenny, taking her arm. 'How about some coffee? You haven't seen the office since it was redecorated, have you?'

He virtually pushed her out of the fabric department, giving her time only to say a hasty, ' 'Bye,' to Doris. Then the two of them were out in the shade of the walkway canopy, where he released her arm.

'So what's the hurry?' Jenny asked, perplexed. 'Something wrong with my talking to Doris?'

'Only that she's busy. Had you been there long?'

'Five minutes or so. Why? What might she have said that you don't want me to hear?'

His face was giving nothing away. 'I don't know what you mean.'

'And I don't believe you!'

They stood facing each other, animosity bristling between them. Adam was never relaxed with her. He had something on his mind, something he was hiding. She was sure of it.

'You'd better tell me, Adam.'

'There's nothing to tell. You're being paranoid. You're still unsettled, which is hardly surprising. You should have stayed quietly at home, as I told you to.'

'I'm old enough to decide for myself whether I'm well enough to be out,' she said. 'You may be my partner, but you're not my keeper.'

54

His eyes glinted. 'Maybe not, but someone has to keep an eye on you. Come on, let's go and have that coffee.'

As he again laid hold of her arm, Jenny wrenched it away. 'Don't keep touching me!'

Adam said nothing, though his mouth tightened and indented cynically at one corner.

Suddenly Jenny couldn't bear the tension any longer. 'Oh, why does it have to be like this?' she sighed. 'After I had that nightmare you were so kind, and now . . .'

'I was just playing white knight to your damsel in distress. I'd have done the same for any frightened child.'

Child. She recognised the rebuff for what it was—an attempt to hurt her. It succeeded. 'I see.'

'What's wrong, Jenny? Can't you bear knowing that I got over you? Did you hope to find me languishing with unrequited love?'

She wished she had never started this conversation. 'If you really want to know, I'm glad you got over it. I've felt awful about the way I . . .'

'Laughed,' he supplied. 'Well, from where I stand now I have to agree that it was pretty laughable. I'm thankful it turned out the way it did. It was a narrow escape.'

Aware of the sting of tears behind her eyes, Jenny said, 'Then why do you still hate me?'

The question made him stop, narrowed eyes searching hers; then his expression changed and he sighed. 'I don't hate you. You're the one who said you hated *me*, if you remember. I'd like us to be friends, but I can't accomplish the miracle on my own. I'm not your enemy, Jen. Believe me.'

Miserable, she watched his familiar face, knowing that she wanted to believe him.

'You're all confused,' Adam said. 'You should never have come here, not so soon. I can't understand why Louise let you use the car.'

'I didn't give her much choice.'

Adam smiled wryly. 'I can imagine. You're too headstrong for your own good. Still, now that you're here . . .' He reached for her arm, hesitated and turned the movement into a gesture to her to precede him. 'Let me show you the changes we've made. I hope you'll approve.'

The showrooms had been extended, displaying Hollander furniture in various room settings enlivened by house plants and the strategic placing of magazines, so that the rooms looked lived in. There was also a new receptionist, a young girl with startling orange hair and so much black liner round her eyes that she looked like a panda.

'What is she—punk?' Jenny asked as they rode smoothly up in the lift to the next floor.

'Verging on it,' Adam agreed with a grimace. 'Still, she's a worker, unlike some of her generation.'

'You talk as though you were an old man.'

'Sometimes I feel like an octogenarian.'

'And I always thought you were Taurean.'

They shared a smile over the feeble joke and Jenny felt better. Maybe it had been a good thing to clear the air, to put the past away for ever. He had forgiven her, hadn't he?

'After you,' he said as the door slid open. She stepped into a newly-carpeted corridor with teak-faced doors on either side. Past the accounts offices a door bore a discreet sign reading 'Mr J Watkinson.' The name made Jenny pause. This had been Adam's office. Who was Mr J Watkinson?

When she glanced at Adam for explanation he pointed towards the end of the corridor, where her father's suite of offices lay.

'You've moved in there?' she asked, hardly believing it. 'Already?'

'Your father and I had been sharing the office for some time,' Adam said. 'Ever since John Watkinson joined us.'

'John . . . Oh, the accountant—who took over your flat upstairs?'

'Quite.' He led the way into the managing director's outer office, where a secretary sat behind a desk—not the friendly Pamela whom Jenny remembered, but an older, more glamorous woman, whose heady perfume swam around her in clouds. She wore a neat blouse and a tight black skirt which she smoothed over her hips as she rose from her desk smiling expectantly. Jenny disliked her on sight.

'This is Sarah Simmons,' Adam told her. 'Sarah, this is Jenny Hollander.'

The woman put on a look of commiseration. 'How do you do, Miss Hollander. We are all so sorry about your father.'

'Would you bring some coffee?' Adam asked, leading Jenny to the inner office.

'Of course, Mr Carfield. Right away.'

The inner sanctum had been completely redecorated. Instead of panelled walls and plain furnishings, with her father's old desk set centrally, the room now had textured oatmeal wallpaper with matching vertical blinds, and a huge desk angled across a corner between the windows. More leather chairs stood round a glass-topped coffee table.

It was all so unfamiliar that Jenny felt disorientated.

'What do you think?' Adam asked.

'I'm not sure. It's more up-to-date, but . . . I thought Dad preferred it old-fashioned.'

'He did, until I convinced him that we needed to keep up with the times. Customers go on impressions. If we presented a fuddy-duddy image, they'd probably expect fuddy-duddy service. Hasn't your millionaire got all the latest office equipment?'

'Of course. I agree with you entirely. It's just . . . I hadn't expected it. And that secretary!

58

about that. It was a call I've been waiting for.'

'I know you're busy. That's why it seems rather strange . . .' She let the sentence hang for a second. 'It seems strange that, being so busy, you have time to play messenger-boy. Surely even a message from the Dowager Lady Granton could have been relayed to Doris over the phone?'

The shutters were down on his face again. 'It could have been.'

Jenny caught her breath in anger. 'Don't lie to me, Adam! The message was just an excuse. You saw me arrive. You came rushing to intercept me.'

'Only because I was concerned about you. You should never have been driving that car.'

She leaned on the desk, staring at him with her mind whirling. 'I wish I could believe you. But it wasn't that way at all. You came to find me because you were afraid of what I might find out. Isn't that the truth?'

'Look, Jenny . . .' Slowly, he came out of his chair and round the desk to take her by the shoulders, his fingers firm and reassuring. 'Why do you imagine I'd lie to you? What is there for me to lie about? You're still in shock. Your father's death, and then the train crash . . . You're not thinking straight. Look at me.'

Unwillingly, she lifted her eyes to meet grey ones that looked back with only sincere concern. This is Adam, she thought. I have no reason to mistrust him. My father thought the world of him.

But her mother had called her father a gullible old fool who would be taken for a ride by the 'paragon' he had employed.

'Well?' Adam prompted.

She dropped her head, staring at his tie. 'Maybe you're right.'

'So why don't you go home and rest? There's nothing you can do here. Let me take care of things.'

She no longer knew what was real and what imaginary. All her instincts were crying out for respite and there was a part of her that wished Adam would take her in his arms and let her lean on him. He was so close she could feel his warmth. If only she could talk to Warren!

Warren. The thought of him cleared her mind. What was she doing longing for Adam's arms when she loved someone else?

She lifted her hands and eased free of him, not looking at him as she moved away, saying, 'You're right, I'd better go home. I'll see you later.'

Escaping through the perfumed outer office, she ignored Sarah Simmons' curious stare. Her head and heart were pounding, her breath short. She felt as though she had narrowly escaped some awful danger. But what was it she feared? Was it Adam himself, his possible duplicity? Or was it her own physical response to him?

Oh, that wasn't true! How could it be true

when she was going to marry Warren Oxenford? What on earth was wrong with her?

CHAPTER FOUR

Resting on her bed that afternoon, Jenny fell into a sleep from which she woke with a clearer head. Outside her window birds sang and the long May evening was beginning with breezy sunlight. Voices reached her as people walked the dale, everything seeming so normal that she wondered why she had ever entertained unfounded suspicions. Adam must be right: she was unsettled and starting to imagine things.

She was about to get dressed when Louise came to say that there was a phone call for her, person to person from the States. Throwing on a dressing-gown, Jenny hurried down the stairs to the study.

'Hello, Jenny?' came Warren's welcome voice.

She sank into a chair, sighing, 'Warren! Oh, how lovely to hear your voice!'

'Something wrong?' he asked. 'Honey, are you okay? Maria said you'd called. She made it sound like it was urgent.'

'Yes. I'm sorry. It's just that I've been trying to reach you for days and . . . I guess I panicked a little. Are you okay? Where are you?'

'Still in New York. Up to my ears in meetings, but it's going pretty well. I should be

64

home in a week or so. What about you?'

'There's an awful lot to clear up. I've hardly started.'

'Well, take your time. Don't even think of coming back until you're good and ready. I know how much there'll be to do. Took me months to sort everything out after Joanie died.'

Months? Was he telling her to stay away for months? 'Warren . . . I talked to Peter a few days ago. Is it true that I've become an embarrassment to you?'

The silence seemed endless. 'Let's not talk about that now, honey,' he said at last. 'Just you concentrate on squaring things over there. When you've got the whole picture we'll talk again.'

'Is there any chance of your coming to England?' she asked, half desperately. 'I really need your advice.'

'Don't you have a family lawyer? Jenny, I've a lot on my mind right now. You're a big girl. You can handle it.'

'Suppose I can't?' She could hardly believe this was Warren speaking—Warren who over the past few years had always rallied to help her. 'What's happened since I left? What has Peter been saying?'

'Honey, I'm tired,' he replied. 'I'm not sleeping too good. I'm in the middle of long hard business discussions that are proving dicey. I'm sorry I can't be there, but it's out of the question. Talk to your lawyer. Do what you think is best. Believe in yourself.'

'Are you all right?' she asked. 'You sound . . . You're not ill?'

'I told you, I'm tired. That's all it is. Listen, I have to go now. I've got more meetings today. You take care of yourself now. I'll talk to you again soon.'

Something had happened, she was sure of it. In her absence, Peter had been working on his father, poisoning Warren's mind against her. Only a week ago, when she left Connecticut, Warren had said he would miss her; now he sounded as though he wouldn't care if he never saw her again. But he had problems of his own. Why should he come running every time she needed advice? She had no right to make demands on him.

But who else could she turn to? All at once she felt utterly alone.

For her meeting with the solicitor that evening she put on a simple black dress, accessorising it with a gold necklet and ear-rings which her father had sent the previous Christmas. Reaching for the emerald ring, she hesitated. Had she misunderstood Warren's references to a shared future, his talk of honeymoon cruises and houses they might buy? No, he had certainly had marriage on his mind, but apparently he was no longer so sure. That being so, she couldn't keep wearing his ring on her left hand. Nor could she suddenly

66

appear with it on her right hand.

She compromised by leaving the ring off altogether.

By the time Adam came home she was in the sitting-room, with Gem at her feet. The dog flew out of the room as soon as the main door opened and Jenny heard Adam speak fondly to him before his footsteps sounded on the parquet, making for the stairs. Seeing her through the open doorway, he stopped to ask, 'How are you feeling?'

Adrift, she thought, but said aloud, 'Better. I had a nap.'

He came into the room, brief-case in one hand, his suit jacket slung over his shoulder. Slowly, he let his glance roam over her, as if he was thinking it a little late for her to go into mourning.

Reacting to the imagined criticism, she said stiffly, 'It's for Mr Wickham. My father always said he hated people wearing black, but Mr Wickham might not understand that.'

Expressionless grey eyes rested on her face. 'If you must know, I was thinking how much it suited you.'

The compliment disconcerted her and it was probably just as well that Adam had turned and left the room before he could see her blush like a schoolgirl. Compliments from him were not what she expected.

Over dinner, she asked what time the solicitor was expected.

'Around eight-thirty,' Adam said. 'I invited him to dine with us, but he had a prior engagement.'

Once again he was taking charge. How dare he presume to think of inviting someone to dinner at her father's house?

'Anyway,' he added, 'it shouldn't take long.'

'Won't that depend on what I want to ask him?'

'He's only coming to tell you what's in the will. It's quite straightforward.'

'You mean . . . you know what he's going to say?'

'I only know what your father told me,' Adam corrected. 'But if you don't mind I'd rather have James Wickham inform both of us officially. There's no reason to worry.'

'I'm not worried, I'm just . . . I'm not looking forward to it, I suppose. It all seems so horribly final.'

'Death is final. It's one of the things we all have to face.'

Without warning, her throat constricted, turning her voice to a croak. 'I know. And I'm a big girl now, I can handle it, just do what I think is best and believe in myself.'

'What?'

Jenny shook herself. 'Nothing. Just something Warren said.'

'I gathered from Louise that you'd heard from him. What did he have to say? Is he coming to take you home?'

68

She bit her lip hard, shaking her head, unable to answer. The trickle of tears threatened to burst into a flood as she muttered, 'Excuse me,' and ran from the room, not knowing where she was heading.

She fled through open french windows and into the garden where shadows lengthened across lawns and terrace. Gem appeared from somewhere, bounding beside her as if he thought this a new game. When she stopped by the lily pond he poised beside her expectantly.

'Oh, go away, Gem!' she croaked.

'Gem!' Adam's stern voice snapped from behind her. 'Come here, boy. Here!'

The dog turned away. Angrily, Jenny wiped tears from her face and took a deep breath. Tears were so futile. They helped nothing. She was an adult woman and it was time she learned to cope alone.

A breeze ran among the trees beyond the wall, stirring the water in the lily pond so that big round leaves moved gently. The stone mermaid stared at Jenny, its face pocked with yellow lichen, its tail curled under it.

After a while, she heard someone coming across the grass. Adam said, 'I've shut Gem in the house. Do you want to talk?'

'There's nothing to say,' she replied, her face averted.

'You're not wearing your ring tonight,' he observed. 'What happened? Did you and Warren have words?'

She drew a deep, painful breath and let it out on a sigh. 'No.'

'You mean I should mind my own business?'

She glanced briefly over her shoulder. 'I didn't say that, Adam. I just prefer not to talk about it right now. I'll be all right. I'm sorry I made such a scene. I keep making scenes. I can't think what's wrong with me.'

'Grief does funny things to people,' he said, a hand gently turning her towards him. He tipped up her face and began to wipe away the traces of tears with a corner of his handkerchief. 'Perhaps you're expecting too much of yourself. There's no need to be ashamed about crying for someone you loved.'

Watching him, she studied the sweep of dark hair framing a face that was so familiar to her it was difficult to view it objectively. A strong face, undoubtedly, with high cheek-bones and deep-set eyes, and a mouth that was neither full nor thin but well-shaped, intent now with concentration as he worked delicately to remove smudged mascara from her cheek. She saw a pulse beating in the side of his throat. He was very close, only inches away.

Torn by an almost unbearable longing to sway nearer, she shut her eyes tightly, clenching every muscle, willing her senses to stop reacting to him.

'It's all right,' Adam said, and drew her quietly into his arms.

Weakened by despair, she leaned on him and let the tears come, weeping for her father, for her spoiled-brat behaviour, for her loss of Warren . . . Her emotions were in disarray. She only knew that she had needed someone to lean on and Adam was there.

When the storm had subsided she remained where she was, relaxed against him with her head tucked under his chin. He was so warm and strong, so comforting. Memories of a golden summer came vividly to her mind, days full of fun, evenings heady with mutual awareness, shared embraces, kisses sweet and exciting.

'Mr Wickham will be here soon,' Adam said in an odd, low voice.

Jenny lifted her head, but whatever she might have said was stopped by the look in his eyes. For a moment they stared at each other, held immobile by that frank meeting of glances, then he drew back, almost tearing himself away from her.

'You ought to go and wash your face,' he said.

She took her cue from him, making believe nothing had happened. It was safer that way, though her heart twisted nervously every time she remembered what she had read in his eyes. It had looked like naked desire. And just what had her own face revealed?

James Wickham arrived promptly at eight-thirty, when Jenny was still in her room fixing her make-up. She found the two men in the sitting-room behind a closed door, talking in low voices which ceased the moment she touched the door handle. As she went in, the solicitor rose politely from his chair and greeted her gravely, conveying his condolences in cultured tones.

He was tall and thin, bald but for two wisps of grey hair above his ears, and he affected half-moon spectacles over which he peered with mild blue eyes. It gave him a faintly disapproving air, though Jenny decided this was just his manner.

'Your father was a good friend of mine,' he told her when they were seated, herself and Adam three feet apart on the settee. 'It's a great loss to us all. I suggest we get this over as quickly as possible. I could read you the entire will, but you won't want to be bothered with all that legal jargon. I'll leave a copy with you, Mr Carfield, since you're the executor.'

'Yes, that's fine,' Adam said,

'And you, Miss Hollander?'

'That's fine with me, too.' She felt tense, wishing it was all over.

'So . . .' the solicitor spread long pale hands. 'The gist of the matter is that apart from a few minor bequests—a small sum of money for Miss Glenford, and so forth—you are your father's sole heir. Everything he had will be yours, in the fullness of time. Of course, these things do take time. Probate has to be granted

72

and all that. May I suggest that you leave it all to myself and Mr Carfield? We can send you the necessary papers for your signature.'

Somehow it had all happened too fast for Jenny to take it in. Was that all there was to it? 'I'm not sure I understand.'

'There's really no need for you to stay in England until the will is proved. It could take months to work out the final details.'

Months. Warren had said the same. She couldn't seem to think straight. 'But I have to decide what to do. About the house, and the business.'

'That can all be dealt with later. By letter, or on the phone. You aren't expected to make important decisions, especially at this difficult time. But your life now is in America. I understand that you're engaged to be married. It will be simpler if you cut your ties here, sell up and use the capital to secure your future.'

Take the lawyer's advice, Warren had said. But Mr Wickham didn't know one vital thing—she was *not* engaged to be married, though she could hardly explain that to him now. 'Is that what you really think I should do? Sell Yethfall House? And Hollander's?'

James Wickham looked gravely at her over his spectacles. 'What would be the point of holding on to them? Pure sentiment? I honestly believe that if your father were here he would agree with me. All that remains here is memories, and those you will have wherever you go.'

That was true, she thought. But her future was not as settled as she had imagined.

'Mr Wickham's right, Jenny,' Adam said. 'Why complicate your life by hanging on to things that belong in the past? Don't think we're trying to get rid of you. You're welcome to stay as long as you like, but in the end America is where you belong now. With Warren.'

She turned on him, green eyes blazing in her pale face. 'It's very kind of you to tell me I'm welcome in my father's . . . in *my* house, but nothing's been decided yet. I need time to think.'

His face had shuttered again, allowing her no hint of his thoughts. 'You're right, of course. I'm sorry. Take all the time you want.'

'I shall!' she flung at him, rising from her seat with all the dignity she could muster. 'Thank you, Mr Wickham. It was kind of you to come out here at this time of night. Please do go ahead with whatever needs to be done. I'll be here if you need me to sign anything. Now if you'll excuse me . . .'

They *were* trying to get rid of her, she thought as she made her way upstairs. If such a thought was not in their minds, why had Adam denied it? Both of them had advised her, urged her, to go away; Mr Wickham had even said her father would have concurred in that. She couldn't believe it. Give up everything he

74

had worked for, everything he had entrusted to her? Whatever they said, it wasn't that easy.

She had only just begun to understand how much it all meant to her. In her mind, home had always been Yethfall House. She had been given no choice about leaving when she was nine years old—the courts had decided she must stay with her mother—but wherever her mother had taken her in the States her heart had always stayed in Derbyshire. For Warren's sake she might have given it up, but she was no longer sure of Warren and without him little remained in Connecticut—an apartment, which was rented, and a few acquaintances. She had never been good at making close friends.

But here in England there was Louise; there was a lovely house where she belonged; there was the countryside she loved, the dale and the stream, the familiar towns. There was a chance to take up a career she had often dreamed of following. And—though she hardly dared admit it to herself—there was Adam.

Such thoughts turned over and over in her mind as she sat on the window-seat and watched the sky flame with sunset. She saw James Wickham leave after half an hour—presumably Adam had invited him to have a drink, playing host again. Oh, why did she have to keep taking offence at everything he did? He was only trying to help, wasn't he?

Shortly afterwards, Adam arrived at her

door to ask if she fancied taking a walk along the dale with him and Gem. Whatever Jenny had expected, it certainly wasn't that.

'Oh . . . why, yes. Do I have time to change?'

'Of course. I want to get out of this suit myself. I'll see you downstairs in five minutes.'

'Fine,' she said, and hurried to change from her black dress into jeans and a white sweat-shirt.

Warm twilight filled the dale, with streaks of pink and gold painted across the sky. Swallows swooped from the trees to dart over the trout stream hawking for flies, their high twittering clear in the quiet evening. Below Yethfall House the valley opened out, passing over a hump of ground with bare outcrops of rock formed into smooth steps high above the stream.

'Take care here,' Adam advised. 'When it's dry, it's slippery.'

'Yes, I remember,' she replied, stepping with care over rock worn shiny by countless feet.

Beyond that obstacle, the dale sloped down in undulating steps, with the stream on the right running over a series of small weirs. Gem raced ahead chasing a stick which Adam kept hurling, and Jenny found herself going back in time.

Of course there had been no Gem six years ago, but she and Adam had often walked in the dale of an evening, finding much to talk and laugh about. Sometimes her father had come with them, but more often he had sent them off alone together while he waited to pour drinks when they came in. He had done everything he could to encourage her relationship with his young associate.

'Penny for them,' Adam said, wrenching her back to the present. He had been watching her, she realised.

'Not worth it. I wasn't thinking much at all, just enjoying the dale. I'm only just beginning to realise how home-sick I've been.'

'That's nostalgia, Jenny. You can't live in the past.'

'So I should go away and leave all of this?' she enquired with a sidelong glance at him.

'In your own best interests, yes. I don't know what sort of tiff you had with your millionaire, but you'll make it up with him.'

'I wish I could be sure of that. And will you please stop calling him "my millionaire"? As far as I know, he's not, except maybe on paper. And he's not mine, either. We . . .' she hesitated, knowing the time for truth had come. 'We never were engaged.'

'What?!' He halted, frowning at her. 'Then who gave you that ring?'

'*He* did! But it wasn't an engagement ring. It was just a gift—to remind me he was there, so he said. When I was in hospital, the nurse put it on the wrong hand.'

'And you kept it there? Why?'

Peering at him under her lashes, she asked herself the same question and found she had no answer. 'I don't know. I wasn't thinking straight. Besides, Warren did want to marry me. He was only waiting for me to be ready. He didn't want to rush me.'

'I thought you'd known him for several years.'

'So I have!' Agitated, she flung out her hands. 'Oh, you don't understand, Adam.'

'Then try explaining.'

Jenny moved on, watching the uneven ground under her feet. 'It's Peter who's behind it. He's always been jealous of my relationship with his father. I don't know what he's been saying, but it's obvious that Warren's having second thoughts.'

'So you stopped wearing the ring.'

'I could hardly keep it on after what he said. He more or less told me not to bother him with my troubles.'

Gem had returned to stand splayed over the stick he had dropped. Adam picked it up, hurling it away far down the dale, and the dog shot after it. Jenny followed, thinking bleak thoughts.

'You never told me that Warren Oxenford had been married before,' Adam said from behind her. He stood watching her with hooded eyes, thumbs hooked in the belt loops of the black jeans he wore with a black shirt. 'How old is this son of his?'

'Does it matter?'

'I want to know.'

'I'm not sure, exactly. Twenty-seven, twenty-eight.' He caught his breath. 'Good God! Are you trying to tell me you were intending to marry an old man?'

'He's not old!'

'He must be fifty at least.'

'He's fifty-three, if you must know.'

'And you're twenty-four. Are you crazy?'

'Lots of women marry older men,' Jenny said dully.

'Yes, and in the majority of cases they have strange reasons for it. They need a father-figure, or they're after his money, or they want somebody to protect them from life. Which is it with you?'

'I'm in love with him!'

'So you said. He's attractive, I suppose. Hair transplants and plastic surgery.'

'He doesn't need them.'

'Does he turn you on?' he demanded.

Jenny stepped back, hoping the twilight concealed her flushed face. 'Don't be crude, Adam!'

'What's crude about it? Isn't it one of the facts of life? Answer me, Jenny!'

'Warren is kind,' she said. 'I feel safe with him.'

'Safe?' He came closer, peering at her through the waning light. 'That seems an odd word to use. Safe in what way?'

'In every way. He doesn't make demands on me.'

'He sounds like a benevolent uncle,' Adam said. 'What you're talking about isn't love, Jenny. You're talking about gratitude, and security. Love isn't safe. It's a pain inside that won't let you be. It's an ache that never stops. It doesn't make you feel secure—just the opposite. It takes hold of you and it hurts you, but it's the sweetest pain on earth.'

He sounded as though he knew all about it. 'Is that how you feel about Cathy?'

The question seemed to surprise him. After a moment he made an impatient gesture. 'No, Cathy and I are just friends. But I do know what love feels like. I've been there. Have you?'

What woman had he loved? she wondered, though she daren't ask. She said, 'No. Not the way you mean. I don't want to, either. It sounds like purgatory.'

'It can be heaven, if it's mutual.' He took her by the shoulders, lifting her face, watching her troubled eyes and her tremulous mouth. 'I don't know what it is you think you feel for Warren Oxenford,' he said, 'but . . . Jen . . . Oh, lord, Jen.'

The words came on a sigh that brushed her face in the moment before he bent his lips to hers, tenderly sweet. She swayed towards him, her arms sliding round him. There were tears on her lashes, but she couldn't deny the relief of giving in to emotions she had been fighting for days.

His arms closed round her, drawing her in against him as his lips became more urgent, forcing hers apart with a hunger that excited her. He was not immune to her, whatever he had said.

Then reality swept her like a cooling breeze. She tore her mouth away, but still clung to him, hiding her face from him. 'Don't,' she managed. 'Oh, please don't.'

'Why?' he whispered against her ear. 'What is it you're afraid of? You don't want to give me false impressions, is that it? Don't worry. I'm not the young fool I was six years ago. I'm not asking you to love me. I'm not asking for anything except that we be honest with each other. We can be friends, can't we? Loving friends?'

Loving friends—it was a nice phrase. And it was enough, for now. She tightened her arms about him, pressing her face to his shirt. 'I'd like that.'

CHAPTER FIVE

That night Jenny slept more soundly than she had done for more than a week, and went down in time to join Adam for breakfast. He smiled up at her across the table, laying aside his newspaper.

'You've come just right. I was going to have to pour myself some more coffee. Now you can do it.'

'So what did your last servant die of—overwork?' said Jenny, but she reached for the ceramic pot.

Adam watched her pour two coffees and put the cream and sugar within easier reach. 'I take it black, thanks. What are you trying to do—fatten me up?'

'Heaven forfend!' she responded. 'I don't think a paunch would suit you. I prefer you lean and hungry.'

'Like Cassius?'

'Who?'

Smiling, Adam shook his head. 'I thought you were quoting Shakespeare. But I forgot what an ignoramus you are.'

'I know Hamlet's soliloquy by heart!' Jenny objected. ' "To be or not to be"—wasn't that the question? Not that I ever cottoned to Shakespeare much. He takes too long getting on with the story.'

'Philistine!' he laughed. 'Cassius was in *Julius Caesar*, not *Hamlet*. Anyway, I'd hate you to think I was like him. "Such men are dangerous". Me, I'm a teddy bear. Get on with your breakfast.'

She spread butter thinly on a piece of toast which she then laced with honey. 'You are a teddy bear,' she said, turning troubled eyes on him. 'Have you really forgiven me?'

'For what?'

'For the way I acted six years ago. I was a selfish little brat. But I didn't mean to laugh. It was nerves. I'd never expected—'

'Jenny.' His hand came warm over hers, sending sparks up her arm to unsteady her heart. 'Will you stop worrying about that? I've told you—I got over it long ago. Besides, it was partly my own fault. I behaved like a bull in a china shop.'

'Even so, I'm sorry I hurt you. And I'm sorry for being so suspicious. You were right yesterday—I was starting to get delusions of persecution. I even imagined there was a conspiracy against me—headed by you and Louise.'

His fingers tightened, lacing with hers. 'No one here would do anything to hurt you. Jenny. You must believe that. Of course you're right—when you turned me down that time I was hurt, otherwise I wouldn't have felt so bitter. But I don't feel that way any more. Let's forget about it. And this time I mean it.' He glanced at his watch as if suddenly remembering the time. 'Hell, I'll be late.' He gulped his coffee, left his seat, grabbed his jacket—and paused to look down at her. 'Meet me in town for lunch?'

'I'd love to.'

'Good. The Granton, then. One o'clock. And just drive carefully.'

Cheered by the thought of having lunch with Adam, she decided to go into town early and do some shopping. Louise wanted some groceries from the supermarket and having stowed them safely in the red Scirocco Jenny wandered round the shops. It was a warm, sunny day and early holidaymakers swelled the town's usual population.

Shortly before one o'clock she sat in the deserted lobby of the Granton Arms Hotel off the square, dressed neatly in a navy skirt suit and green blouse. She watched the street for a sight of Adam, feeling oddly nervous, like a schoolgirl before a first date. The clock in the square was striking one when Adam came striding up the steps to the glass doors. His swift smile warmed her.

'You're punctual,' he approved.

'So are you. One thing I hate is being kept waiting.'

'Me, too. Shall we go straight in? I'm going to enjoy being seen with the beautiful Miss Hollander.'

'Seen by whom?' Jenny asked dryly. 'There's

hardly anybody in the dining-room.'

'Then at least we can have some privacy.'

The dining-room had a view through trees to a shady bend of the river, and they were given a table in one of the big bay windows. Jenny remembered dining there a few times with her father.

'Don't look so glum,' Adam pleaded. 'This was intended to take your mind off things, not bring on a fit of the miseries. Why don't you ask me about my morning?'

'How was your morning?'

'Pretty routine. Now what shall we talk about?'

A laugh bubbled out of Jenny. 'You are a fool,' she said fondly. 'Oh, Adam, why have I made such a mess of everything? After mother died, I should have come home, to be with Dad. If I'd known . . .'

'But you didn't know. It's no good thinking like that. Things are as they are. Did he ever ask you to come home permanently?'

'No, not in the last few years. He was too caring to try to influence me. But it was always what he hoped for.'

'You could be wrong. Your life's moved on. He knew that. Have you thought about what you're going to do?'

'Yes, on and off. I still can't decide. Mr Wickham was so definite when he told me to sell up.'

'Well, it would be the sensible thing. You've

made a life in America now. You've got a lot of friends, so you said, and a good job, and an apartment.'

'My "friends" would hardly miss me. I've always been an outsider. Partly through my own choice—I don't easily get close to people. My apartment is just a few rooms where I happen to keep my belongings. And as for my job . . . with things as they are, I can hardly go on working as Warren's personal assistant.'

'Have you decided not to marry him?'

She stared at him in surprise. 'I thought we went through all that last night.'

'You might have had second thoughts. What if he comes over here and wants to take you back? Would you go?'

'Would you want me to?'

'It's not for me to decide,' Adam said. 'I said my piece last night.'

'And I listened. Marrying Warren would be running away from life. In hospital, when I suddenly realised how alone I was, I thought it was the answer. But panic is no reason for marrying someone.' Her path now seemed clear. Somehow the decision had been made for her. 'I'm going to stay here. This is where I belong.'

She had expected him to show pleasure, but instead he was wearing that unreadable mask again. 'In England, you mean.'

'I mean here—in Derbyshire, in Yethfall Dale. I'll live in Yethfall House, and . . . I'll do what I've always wanted to do—work at Hollander's.'

The idea seemed to bother Adam. A furrow drew his brows together. 'It's not that easy.'

'Why isn't it? My father always hoped that some day—'

'Pipe-dreams,' Adam broke in.

Jenny's brow creased as she stared at him. 'I thought you'd be pleased. You said you cared about my father. Won't you help me fulfil his last wishes?'

That reached him, she could see. 'His last wish was for you to be happy.'

'I *shall* be happy, here in Derbyshire where I belong. Please don't argue with me, Adam. I've made up my mind. I'm staying. And I'm going to find a way to make myself useful at Hollander's. After all, if I'm the majority shareholder I have a right to make some of the decisions. Don't I?'

For a split second she thought she saw despair in his eyes, but she must have imagined it because the next moment he was reaching for her hand and smiling at her. 'Of course you do. Okay, if you're absolutely sure, I'll do everything I can to help.'

'You will!? Adam, that's wonderful! I was beginning to think I was going to have to fight you all the way.'

'I was playing devil's advocate,' he said, 'just to convince myself you were serious. It's a big step, Jenny.'

'It's what I want.' She was filled with hope and relief. 'I didn't know it until now, but this is what I've always wanted. Can we get started right away? Shall I come back to the office with you?'

'No, not this afternoon. We'll talk about it tonight. You've had enough excitement for one day.'

'I'm not Gem, you know,' she laughed. 'Honestly, I feel just great. I'm raring to go. But . . .' Seeing the stubborn look on his face, she sighed. 'All right, if you insist—friend. But pretty soon you're going to have to stop playing big brother. You don't have to take responsibility for everything just because I'm a woman. You didn't do that when Dad was here, did you?'

Adam searched her face with troubled eyes, saying eventually, 'You'll have to give me time to adjust. It honestly never occurred to me that you would decide to stay.'

'Well, I have. And that's that.' She wrinkled her nose at him. 'You'll just have to get used to working for a woman.'

Filled with dreams of a rosy future, she waited as he paid the bill and then they walked to where she had left her car in the empty cattle-market. There were few people around among the sheds and stalls, but birds picked at scraps and a family of ducks waddled towards the river.

The sight of the piping ducklings made

Jenny laugh. 'Look at them, Adam. Aren't they gorgeous?'

'What?'

'The baby ducks!' But the frown on his face wiped away her smile. 'What's wrong? You don't mind that I'm going to be your boss, do you? It's only on paper. Hollander's is doing just fine under your management. I'll be happy to leave it that way. It won't make any difference to us, will it? Will it, Adam?'

She laid a hand on his sleeve, looking anxiously up into his face, and he laid his arm round her shoulders, pressing her to his side.

'No, of course it won't. And thanks for the vote of confidence.'

'You are pleased that I'm staying, aren't you?'

In the moment before he replied, he let his glance sweep over her face, the furrow slowly leaving his brow. 'Of course I'm pleased,' he said at last, and bent to brush a kiss across her mouth.

Shocks of pleasure ran through her, making her wide-eyed as she gazed up at him. But voices made them draw apart, glancing to where a young couple with two children were coming back loaded with shopping to the car-park.

Jenny shared a rueful glance with Adam. 'I'd better go,' he said. 'I'll see you tonight. Drive safely.'

'And you,' she replied, watching him walk

away with eyes that admired every lean, elegant line of him. She felt happy, as she had never felt before.

She had come home, and Adam was here.

Returning to Yethfall House, Jenny was drawn to the kitchen by the smell of baking cakes. Louise was busy mixing another batch, a smear of flour on her face.

'I have some news, Louise,' Jenny announced, 'I'm not going back to America.'

Louise stared at her, the wooden spoon pausing. Glancing at Jenny's bare left hand, she said, 'What about your Mr Oxenford?'

'That's all off. It was never really on, to tell you the truth. So . . . I'm going to stay, Louise. I'm going to stay here and work at Hollander's. I hope you'll stay on and keep house for me.'

Louise was gaping at her incredulously. 'You mean—here, at Yethfall House? But . . . what about Mr Carfield?'

'What about him? Good heavens, men and women share apartments these days, never mind a huge house like this. I don't doubt it will cause some comment in provincial Derbyshire, but . . . Louise, there's no need to look so shocked. This is not the nineteenth century.'

Louise snapped her mouth shut, though her expression remained stunned. 'Does he know?'

'Who—Adam? Of course he knows. We discussed it over lunch. It was always on the cards, you know. Why was everybody so sure

I'd be content to pack up and go back to the States?'

'We just thought . . . that you'd want to. Especially when you were going to marry an American.'

'Well, I'm not going to marry Warren. That's one thing I'm sure of. I belong here. My home is here. My father always wanted me to come back. You must know that.'

Looking down into the mixing bowl, Louise said, 'Your father had a lot of dreams that never came true. This last few years . . . I don't believe he really thought you'd ever come home to stay, except . . .'

'Except?' Jenny prompted.

'Oh, it was his fondest dream.' The housekeeper gazed into the distance. 'That you and Mr Carfield would get together and live happily ever after. He often used to talk about that. All of you here together, and your children on his knee.' She sighed, shaking her head. 'Castles in the air.'

'I wonder,' Jenny said, and left the housekeeper to ponder on that.

Going out to the garden with Gem at her side, she saw a woman walking down the drive. The stranger was dressed in a tweed jacket and a long cotton skirt, carrying a crash helmet and what looked like a bunch of flowers wrapped in blue paper. She was in her thirties, very tall and rather plump, with dishevelled dark hair which she kept stroking from her face as the wind caught in its strands.

Someone to see Louise, Jenny thought, but then Gem barked and went streaking away to bound round the newcomer in welcome. The woman bent to pat him and Jenny started toward the pair, curious.

'Hello.'

The newcomer looked up, her glance flicking over Jenny as she straightened, smiled and held out her hand. 'You must be Jenny Hollander. I'm Cathy Brent.'

Trying to hide her surprise, Jenny put on a smile, shaking the proffered hand. 'You're Adam's friend. I'm glad to know you.'

'You too.' Her eyes were inquisitive, probing. 'Thought I'd come over and say hello. Hope you don't mind. Oh—these are for you. Tulips. Got a bit battered on the bike.'

'How kind. Thank you. You came by push-bike?'

'Motor-bike,' Cathy said. 'I left it up in the village. This hill's a bit too steep for the old girl. By the way, I was sorry to hear about your father. He was a nice man.'

'You knew him?' Jenny asked.

'I met him a few times, when I came here with Adam.'

'Then you must know Louise, too. Shall we go inside and ask her if she'll make a cup of tea? Come on, Gem.'

Leading the way into the house, Jenny wondered at the purpose of this visit.

Somehow the vicar's daughter was not what Jenny had expected, not the sort of woman who seemed likely to attract Adam, though he had said she was "just a friend".

Inviting her visitor to sit down, Jenny went to ask Louise to make tea. By the time she returned, Cathy had made herself at home, sitting on the settee fondling an enamoured Gem.

'Tea won't be long.' Jenny perched on the edge of a chair feeling ill at ease. 'I gather you've been in Shadwell about two years. How do you like it?'

'Very much, though the vicarage isn't all that convenient. Still, the kids love the space.' Noting Jenny's surprise, she explained, 'I'm divorced. I have two children—Sam and Sally. My father's a widower, so I keep house for him.'

'Oh, I see,' Jenny said. 'Did the children go to lunch with you on Sunday? I know Adam must have enjoyed his day. He came in whistling like a blackbird.'

Cathy laughed. 'He spent most of the time with Dad, talking antiques. I think you've got the picture a bit wrong. Adam and I are friends. We do go out together sometimes, but only because we're both lonely. And that suits me. I'm not ready to get involved again.'

Obviously her divorce had left scars. Jenny found herself warming to the vicar's daughter.

Louise came in with a tea-tray, smiling and

greeting Cathy as an old friend. She also brought the tulips in a vase which she set on the coffee table before departing and taking Gem with her.

Jenny picked up the teapot. 'Milk and sugar?'

'Yes, thank you. I—er—gather you're planning to return to America fairly soon.'

'Not any more. No, I'll be staying, all being well.' She looked up as a thought struck her. 'Does that bother you?'

'Far from it,' Cathy replied with a smile. 'I know Adam will be delighted. You know, of course, that he's in love with you.'

The tea spilled into the saucer Jenny set the pot down, aware that she was flushing. 'Oh, really . . . !'

'Sorry.' Cathy pursed her lips into a moue of regret. 'I do tend to speak my mind too freely, so they're always telling me, but you have a right to know. Right from the start I sensed a deep sadness in him. I couldn't understand why a man like that should be lonely. Then he dropped a photograph from his wallet one day. He tried to hide it, but I saw it, and when I asked him about it I could tell he still cared for the girl in that picture. Only he'd lost her, somehow. I thought she must be dead, until last week, when you were unconscious in hospital and he was worried half to death. I'm afraid I came today to satisfy my curiosity. I wanted to know if you were the same girl who was in that photo. And of course you are.'

Love isn't safe, Adam had said. *It's an ache that never stops.* Could it be true that the woman for whom he felt such pain was Jenny herself?

'Don't you think it's a bit disloyal of you to be telling me this?' she asked.

'Probably so,' said Cathy with a grin. 'But I still think you've a right to know. From what I know of Adam, it'll take him ages to get round to telling you himself.'

The conversation with Cathy haunted Jenny for the rest of the afternoon, coupled with vague disquiet as she recalled Louise's odd reaction to the news that she was staying. She could hardly wait to talk to Adam. When she heard the car she went out onto the terrace and walked across to the garage, with Gem running ahead of her.

'Hello, you great soft fool,' she heard Adam greeting the dog. 'Get out of the way, idiot.' He was removing his brief-case from the car but paused at sight of her. 'Well, hello. What's this? A reception committee?'

'We're just glad to see you,' Jenny said. 'Do you mind?'

'On the contrary. But if it happens too often I might get to expect it. You all right? You look a bit . . . What's wrong? Did Warren phone again?'

'No, it's . . . it's nothing, really. Cathy Brent was here.'

Immediately, he turned wary. 'What did she want?'

'Just to say hello. I like her. And she did say . . . something about a photograph you keep in your wallet?'

'Oh,' he said flatly. 'I had a feeling she might . . . Damn it, she had no right to tell you about that.'

'Then it's true? You hung onto that photo, despite everything?'

She could see the answer in his face. 'I kept it because it was all I had left. Well, is it really such a surprise? Okay, so I'm a damn fool, but there's nothing I can do about it. You don't have to worry. I know you don't feel the same.'

'How can you be so sure?' she asked in a low voice.

'I just know. You need somebody and right now I'm it. That's not the same. Don't kid yourself, Jenny. Or me. Not even you can be that cruel twice.'

With that, he swung past her and made for the house, with Gem at his heels.

Feeling that she couldn't go into the house yet, Jenny set out for a walk along the wild dale. She crossed the stream at stepping-stones and went on through bracken and long grasses, deep in thought. She lost track of time. She climbed stretches of rock; more than once she slipped, and thought that she was going to fall and injure herself far from hope of rescue. Then the rain started, when she was miles out

96

in open countryside, wishing she hadn't come so far. Her strength was already failing. Finally she reached a road and followed it on through drenching rain and fading daylight until she reached Yethfall village.

It was almost dark as a bruised and battered Jenny limped the last few yards down the lane into Yethfall Dale, quivering with near-exhaustion. She had hardly enough strength to open the gate and walk up the drive. Holding on to the balustrade, she dragged herself up the steps and half fell through the door. As she hung there, shaking, she heard Louise say, 'Oh, dear God! Mr Carfield. *Mr Carfield!*'

Jenny was aware of Adam appearing in a hurry. Swearing, he swept her up in his arms and she felt herself being conveyed up the stairs.

'Is she all right?' Louise's voice seemed to come through mists.

'How the hell do I know?' Adam snarled, taking Jenny into her bedroom.

'Not on the bed!' Louise gasped. 'Put her in the chair. Let me deal with her. Mr Carfield, please! It's not right that—'

'Then for God's sake *do* something!'

'Get me some towels,' Louise said, patting Jenny's face. 'Jenny! Jenny, can you hear me?'

'Yes, I hear you,' Jenny muttered, shaking. 'Oh, I'm so cold!'

'We'll soon have you warm. Oh—thank you. And now, please, Mr Carfield, will you leave us?'

'Shall I phone the doctor?' Adam said.

Jenny roused herself a little. 'No need for that,' she managed through chattering teeth. 'I'm just wet and c-c-cold.'

'Damn you, Jenny!' he flung at her. 'You're still a spoiled brat. What did you mean by running off that way? Have you any idea what hell we've been going through? Or was that the plan—to make me suffer?' He must have pushed Louise aside for Jenny felt his hands fasten on her shoulders, shaking her. 'You're a stupid, childish, impossible—'

'Mr Carfield!' Louise sounded shocked. 'Not now!'

He growled under his breath and a moment later Jenny winced as the door slammed.

'He's worried about you, that's all,' Louise said. 'Come on, let's get you out of these wet things.'

*   *   *

Jenny woke to hear rain still pattering against her window, though full daylight had come. She was still and sore, and when she moved pains led her to discover bruises on several parts of her anatomy.

She drew the covers back round her as someone tapped on the door.

'It's only me,' said Louise, bringing a breakfast tray arranged with a tiny vase of lily

98

of the valley. 'How are you this morning?'

'I feel like I tangled with a steamroller, but I guess I'll live. That breakfast smells good.'

'Well, you didn't have any dinner last night,' the housekeeper said. 'Neither did Mr Carfield, come to that. Whatever possessed you to go off that way?'

'I just needed to walk, to get rid of too much adrenalin. Louise, I'm sorry if I worried you. Is Adam still angry?'

'Hard to tell. He didn't say much this morning, just drank a cup of coffee and went off to work. Oh—there's the phone. Excuse me.'

The breakfast occupied most of Jenny's attention and by the time Louise returned she had emptied the tray.

'That was the best meal I've had in ages,' she sighed. 'Who was on the phone?'

Louise avoided her eyes, busying herself with the tray. 'Mr Carfield, wanting to know how you were. Well, I have things to do. Perhaps you'd better stay in bed for a while. See how you feel.'

Staying in her room suited Jenny. She needed to think. She sat on her window-seat with a velvet wrap over her nightgown as she stared at the dripping rain.

Lately her life had turned upside down and she could no longer trust her own feelings. Yesterday she had been convinced that she was falling in love with Adam, but only a few days

99

ago she had been equally convinced that she loved Warren Oxenford. Her emotions were all in a muddle because of her father's death, because of Warren's desertion, and because of her guilt over the way she had treated Adam six years before. It was hardly the time to make decisions which would affect her whole life.

A tap on the door made her say, 'Come in, Louise.'

'It's not Louise,' said Adam's voice.

Heart thudding, she watched him close the door and stand there regarding her wretchedly. His hair was damp, the shoulders of his grey suit spotted with rain.

'I thought you were at work,' she said. 'I didn't hear the car.'

'I left it outside the gate. How can I work, Jenny? I've been trying, but my mind won't stay on it. The tenth time I found myself staring out of the window at nothing I decided it was time I came home. We can't go on like this.'

'Do you think I'm happy?' she asked.

'I know you're not. And I know it's partly my fault. I wish . . . I wish I could go back six years and wipe out what happened. If I hadn't made my move too soon, everything might have been different. You'd have kept coming to visit your father. We'd have gone on getting to know each other. You'd have had time to grow up. Only I couldn't wait. I was afraid that if you went back to the States you'd meet someone else. And so I ruined everything.'

A tiny spurt of hope lit deep inside Jenny, though she refused to let it grow the way it wanted to, to fill all her being. She had made that mistake too often. A small hope was enough for now.

'I think it will be better for both of us if I move out,' Adam said. 'I'll go today, if you want.'

Dismay brought her to her feet. 'That's not what I want. Adam . . . You didn't ruin everything. Between us we made it more difficult, that's all. But we're older and wiser now. Let's take it a step at a time.' She held out her hands to him. 'Loving friends, yes?'

He hesitated, but only for an instant. Three long strides brought him across the room and then he was cradling her against him, his arms hard about her, his face pressed to her hair. 'Oh, yes, Jen!' he whispered. 'Oh, yes!'

They stood holding each other tightly, stroking and touching until their lips met and their embrace deepened into passion and need. Jenny felt herself swept up in the sensual power of the man so close to her, her body melting against him. She leaned on him, gazing up at him as he lifted his head and looked down at her with darkened, possessive eyes.

'A step at a time?' he said gruffly. 'In that case . . .' Releasing her, he stepped away, catching her hands in his. 'In that case, I'll get back to the office before Louise gets the wrong idea.'

She was tempted to delay him, to persuade him to stay, but she had enough sense to know that that might be taking a step too far, as yet. 'Okay. And listen, Adam, since I'm definitely going to be moving back here, I shall have to go to the States to clear things up there. I might as well go as soon as possible and get it over with.'

Adam didn't like the idea. 'Will that mean seeing Warren?'

'That's partly why I must go—I have to talk to him face to face. In case you're wondering, I'll be giving him back that emerald.'

'Maybe I should come with you.'

'That wouldn't be very practical. Besides, I've got to learn to stand on my own two feet. It will only take a few days. I'll see Warren, hand in my resignation, pack up my apartment and arrange to have my things shipped over. Then I'll take the first flight home.' Seeing that he still looked doubtful, she reached to touch his face. 'Don't look like that. A short while apart will help us both see things more clearly. Adam, if there's anyone in the world I've ever loved, apart from my father, it's you.'

Suddenly he was fierce. 'You had better mean that!' he growled, and kissed her so hard that she felt the pressure of his mouth long after he had gone.

CHAPTER SIX

That Adam was not entirely happy about her trip to the States became evident in the few days it took Jenny to make arrangements. Often he seemed to be miles away, thinking bleak thoughts, until she drew him back to the present and he put on a face for her benefit. She guessed that he was worried in case Warren tried to change her mind.

She had decided to stay away from Hollander's until after she had cut her ties in the States. Only then would she be able to put her mind to the future. She spent her days quietly with Louise and Gem, recovering her full strength. Her evenings were filled by Adam's company. They went walking in the dale, or sat talking over drinks after dinner before going to their separate rooms. Jenny wasn't sure whether she was 'in love', but certainly she had never been so close to it before. In Adam's presence she felt safe, and contented.

On the day she was due to leave, Adam drove her all the way to London. She felt edgy and knew she was chattering too much. Perhaps she too was worried about seeing Warren, but she owed it to him to explain in person. At Heathrow, waiting for the flight to be called, they talked mainly of what was on view around them, the hustle of arrivals and departures, the small human dramas and comedies taking place, the variety of dress and nationalities.

When at last the flight to New York was announced, Jenny got to her feet, thumbing the strap of her bag over her shoulder.

'Have you got everything?' Adam asked. 'Ticket? Passport?'

'Yes.' She couldn't look at him. Suddenly she was so uptight she felt sick.

'You'll phone me when you get there, won't you?'

'Of course I will.' Now at last she turned her eyes to his face, seeing him anxious. Emotions rose to engulf her and she threw herself at him. 'Oh, Adam, please be here when I get back.'

His arms enfolded her, his mouth pressed to her ear. 'Of course I'll be here. I'll always be here. Just make sure you do come back. I love you, Jenny.'

'And I love you,' she wept. 'Oh, I do! I do!'

A hand along her cheek made her look at him as for a long moment he searched her eyes, trying to convince himself she was sincere, then he bent to possess her mouth, holding her painfully tight. She replied with equal passion and despair, oblivious to the crowds around them, knowing only that at last she had found the man she really wanted. The next few days stretched empty ahead of her, seeming like years.

*　　　*　　　*

Arriving in Hartford with its bustle of lunch-time traffic was like stepping into another world, familiar and yet alien. Jenny took a cab and as it moved along the streets she wished she had let Adam come with her. She was stupidly afraid that something might happen, that she might never see him again.

Her apartment remained as she had left it—clean and tidy. The furnishings were modern, functional, with plants arranged on a tall stand in one corner. It looked, Jenny thought, just like one of the settings in the Hollander showrooms, except that the furnishings were much less fine. It had never been a real home.

Though it was early afternoon in Connecticut, her body-clock told her it would be evening in England. Adam ought to be home by now. She looked at the phone, feeling a deep need to hear his voice. But so that she should have some news to tell him, she sat down and dialled the number of OxenCo first.

A few moments later, Warren was saying in her ear, 'Jenny! Honey, I'm glad you called. What time did you get back?'

'How did you know I was in Hartford?' she asked.

'I phoned your house in England, first thing this morning, and your housekeeper told me you were on the way home. How's it been, honey? Pretty grim, I guess. Say, I'm sorry about the way I must have sounded the other day. I was feeling low. Missing my sleep, and my girl. But now that you're home—'

'I'm not staying,' she interrupted, disturbed by the pleasure in his voice.

The silence sang in her ear until she wondered if they had been disconnected, then, 'How do you mean?'

'I mean just what I say, Warren. I'd rather not go into it on the phone. I'd like to come in to the office to talk to you.'

'I see,' was all he said.

'Can I get to see you this afternoon, or are you tied up?'

'I was, but I can cancel my appointments. Don't come here, I'll come to your apartment.'

'There's no need—'

'There's every need,' he said. 'What I have to say is better said in private.'

That sounded ominous. Was he going to make things difficult?

She would not phone Adam yet, she decided. First let her get this interview with Warren out of the way. Afterwards she would probably be in need of some reassurance. But she would not let Warren influence her. She would not! Whatever he had to say, she had made up her mind.

Warren Oxenford wore his years lightly. He was of medium height with silver hair and an even tan against which his eyes looked very blue. His athletic frame was clothed in a beautifully-cut business suit with a silk shirt and tasteful tie, and on his little finger he wore a chunky gold ring which he had a habit of twisting when he was agitated. He twisted the ring now, surveying her across the room.

'What happened over there?'

'It's a long story. But the bottom line is that I've realised England is where I belong. I've got ties there that can't be broken. I have a lovely home, a business to run, and . . .' she might as well be totally honest, 'there's a man named Adam Carfield. Seeing him again has changed everything. I'm sorry, Warren. Seems you were right—you often told me I wasn't ready to marry you.'

'Not yet! But I thought the time would come! Who is this guy?'

'He's a colleague of my father's. I've known him for a long time.'

'You never mentioned him before.'

'It wasn't easy to talk about, especially to you. Anyway, it was all over before I ever met you, or so I thought. My father knew better. Apparently he always hoped I'd marry Adam in the end.'

'Is that why you're doing it—because your father wanted it? Hell, Jenny, filial loyalty doesn't stretch that far!'

'That isn't why,' she denied. 'Besides, nothing's been said yet about marriage. It's too soon. But it may well end that way.'

'Is that what you want?'

'Yes, it is.'

Sighing, he sat down on the arm of a chair, staring at the carpet. 'God knows I'm trying to feel glad for you, honey, but I just can't believe I've lost you for good. I should have come over there.'

'I thought you'd washed your hands of me,' Jenny said.

His head snapped up. 'I was fighting for my life, businesswise. I was fighting Peter, because of you, and when that letter came . . . I guess I figured it would be best to get out sooner than give myself more problems.'

'Letter?' she queried. 'What letter?'

Warren heaved himself off the chair and went to stare out of the netted window, fiddling again with his signet ring. 'Maria sent it on to me in New York. It's from your father.'

'You had a letter from my father?' she managed, feeling as though her heart had slowed. 'Why did he write to you? When?'

'A couple days before he died. He wrote because—I guess because there was no one else. He said I'd been a surrogate father to you.' He glanced briefly over his shoulder, his mouth twisting. 'That hit below the belt, though I guess he was right. Anyhow, he said I should encourage you to get together with this Carfield.'

'You mean . . .' she got out, 'he knew he

didn't have much longer?'

'He'd known it for some time.'

'I don't believe you!'

'Then read it for yourself.' A hand dug into an inner pocket and whipped out an envelope which he held out, forcing her to step forward and take it. She retreated to a chair to read it, though the paper trembled in her hand so much that the words were blurred:

'This may be the last letter I shall ever write. I have known for some time now that my illness was incurable, though it is of no importance. I'm tired of a life I have spent with such futility. My only remaining concern is for Jenny, my daughter.

'It will be a shock to her when she hears the news, but I've tried to save her the anguish of knowing what was happening. She would have wanted to be with me and I could not have borne for her to watch me grow feeble. Let her remember me as I was. Tell her I love her very much.

'I know she has great affection for you. It has been a great comfort to me to know she had someone whom she could regard as a surrogate father. I wish to ask you to do what I myself would do, were I able. When I'm gone, will you stand by Jenny and encourage her friendship with Adam Carfield? They are meant for each other, if only they will give themselves a chance to discover it.

'I have so little to give her. If ever she finds out the truth she will be in need of friends. I know Adam is willing, but Jenny may need persuading.

'She is all I have left, Warren. I entrust her to your care.

'Sincerely, Henry Hollander.'

She sat staring at the paper. The letter was written in her father's familiar script, more scrawly than usual but still recognisable. It was dated only two days before he died.

'Adam told me it was sudden,' she whispered. 'So did Louise. At least . . . they let me believe it was sudden. If he was so ill, why didn't they let me know? I ought to have been there.'

'Obviously he didn't want that,' Warren said. 'You read what he felt about having you around when he was sick.'

'He always did try to shelter me from any unpleasantness. He probably told Adam and Louise that I wasn't to know. Oh, that's so like him! But I ought to have known there was something wrong.'

'How? By telepathy? Honey . . .' He started towards her, stopped himself. 'Sorry. I guess I'd better stop calling you that, if you're determined to leave me—if you're bent on going back to some guy you were all through with a couple weeks ago. He worked for your

110

father, you said? The boss's daughter must be a pretty nice catch for him.'

Jenny looked at him from her eye corner. 'I might have known you'd look at it that way. Like your son, you think everything revolves around money. Adam isn't like that. He loves me.'

'Sure he does. He'd be crazy not to, but he sure discovered it in a hurry when you got to be an heiress.'

'Warren, that's a foul thing to say! You don't know the first thing about him. Adam . . .' How she could put into words what she felt about Adam?

'He seduced you,' Warren guessed.

She shot to her feet, outraged. 'I never realised before what a nasty mind you have.'

'Jealousy has a way of doing that to a man,' Warren replied with a gesture that might have been meant as apology. 'Okay, so I know you were never in love with me. That doesn't mean I have to like it when I find myself outmanoeuvred by some guy who had the gall to make his pitch just when you were most susceptible. The whole thing has a nasty smell. Think, honey. Do you really know what you're doing?'

'I know exactly what I'm doing. You won't talk me out of it with unfounded innuendo about someone you've—' The words broke off as a curtain seemed to part in her mind and she sank back into her chair, a hand to her head. 'Oh God, what a fool I was! It was there right in front of me and I never saw it.'

'What?'

She looked up at him, tears misting her sight. 'The reason why Dad stopped driving. The reason he gave up his office and let Adam take over. And why Adam moved into Yethfall House. All the clues were there, and I never bothered to stop and ask about them. They must have thought I was blind.'

'You weren't in any fit state to think straight,' Warren said, kneeling beside her with a comforting hand on her arm. 'You're still in shock. You just lost your father.'

'That's what *they* kept telling me!'

'Well, isn't it the truth?'

With an effort, she controlled herself. 'Maybe you're right. I was in an accident, too. I was unconscious for two days.'

'You what?!'

Seeing him go pale, she laid her hand over his. 'Don't look so worried. It was just a bump on the head. I'm fine now. They kept me in hospital, and after I got out I took it easy. Adam and Louise wouldn't let me do anything else.' Realising that she ought not to be touching him—in fact, did not want to be touching him—she withdrew her hand and moved her arm so that he sat back and stood up, moving away.

Jenny too got up, going to her handbag for a tissue to wipe her face, seeing there the small

112

box in which she kept the emerald ring. She held it in her palm for a moment before turning to him.

'Don't be offended, Warren, but I think I should give you back this ring. I wouldn't feel right keeping it now.'

'It was a gift,' he said. 'From a friend to a friend. I'm not going to step right out of your life, Jenny. We'll keep in touch, and if ever you need me . . .'

'But the ring . . .'

'If you don't want to wear it then save it for a rainy day. If ever you're in need of money . . .'

'I wouldn't feel right about it. Really, Warren—'

With a glint in his eye, he came and took her by the shoulders. 'You want to insult me? Hurt me? You want to cut me right out and pretend this last few years never happened? Is that what Carfield wants—for you to give up all your old friends?'

'No, of course not!'

'Then keep the ring. Allow me that much. It's a token of affection, from a "surrogate father".'

Uncomfortable under his bitter gaze, Jenny looked down at the ring box. 'In that case . . . Thank you. I'll treasure it.'

'Be sure you do,' Warren said, letting his hands linger on her a moment before moving away.

'May I keep the letter, too?'

'If you want. I have a copy.'

Putting the ring into her bag, she returned to pick up the letter, looking sadly at her father's final message. There was so much love in it, so much concern for her.

'Were you going to do what he asked? If it hadn't happened by itself, would you have tried to persuade me to marry Adam?'

'Hell, no! I was keeping out of it, until you made up your own mind. If you'd come back to me, I'd never have shown you that letter.' Seeing her expression, he made an irritable gesture. 'Okay, so it would have been dirty pool, but I'm not looking for sainthood. I'm just a guy who happens to love a girl who doesn't love him. I'll survive it. So long as you're going to be okay with this Carfield.'

'I shall be.' She glanced again at the letter. 'I wonder what he meant . . . *"I have so little to give her. If ever she finds out the truth . . ."* He gave me a great deal—the house, the business . . . Maybe he didn't mean material things. But what truth is there to know?'

'I'd forgotten that part,' Warren said, coming to take the letter from her hand, frowning over it.

'He probably meant my being kept in ignorance of his illness. He knew I'd feel badly about that. There can't be anything else.'

'I'm not so sure.' He looked up, fixing her with narrowed eyes. 'What was that about Carfield moving into the house? When?'

'About a year ago—presumably when it became apparent that Dad wasn't well. Adam said Dad needed company, which was probably true, if not the whole truth.'

'He's still there?'

'Well—yes. I could hardly turn him out, though he did offer to go if I wanted him to.'

'The house belongs to you now?'

What was he getting at? 'Apart from a few small bequests, Dad left everything to me.' Disturbed by the thoughts she could see moving in the sharp brain behind those eyes, she turned aside. 'Don't imagine things, Warren.'

'You saw the will?' When she didn't reply, he turned her to face him, eyes narrowed with suspicion. 'You did see the will?'

'Well, no. There wasn't much point in wading through reams of legal jargon. But Mr Wickham, the solicitor, told me the gist.'

'You should have insisted on reading the will,' Warren said. 'When there's money involved, you have to be sure it's all accounted for, down to the last cent. There's too much jiggery-pokery goes on.'

An incredulous laugh broke out of her. 'We're not talking about millions, you know. Who would try to cheat me? James Wickham? He's the type who would worry himself silly if he found he'd walked off with so much as a pencil that didn't belong to him. I've no doubt that Dad's estate is meticulously accounted for. Mr Wickham would see to that.'

'Just the same, I'll be happier when you've seen the will.'

'Oh, Warren! You're too suspicious. It's all these big deals you're involved in. Hollander Craft Furnishings isn't in the same league with OxenCo. By the way . . . how did it go in New York?'

'It was dodgy for a while. Took some fast talking on my part, but I came through.'

'Then may I assume that you don't want me to work notice?'

He watched her for a moment as if weighing the odds. 'I feel like demanding that you fulfil your contract and work the full month, so I could use the time to wine and dine you and make you forget this Carfield. But I'd be on a loser, wouldn't I?'

'Yes, I'm afraid you would.'

'So I give up gracefully, do I?'

'I'd hate to quarrel with you. I can't tell you how much I've appreciated all your help and support. But it's not gratitude you want, is it?'

'Darn right it's not. But I know when I'm beaten. Okay, just drop me a letter at the office. I'll see you get any salary that's due. And . . .' He tapped her father's letter against his thumb, 'I'll study on my copy of this. Will you let me see you again before you desert me for ever? How about dinner one evening?'

She could hardly refuse such an invitation. 'I'd like that. And Warren . . . thank you for not making difficulties.'

'Don't thank me yet. I may still come up with something.'

When he had gone, she phoned Yethfall House. Adam must have been sitting by the phone for he answered it immediately.

Jenny! Everything all right?'

The sound of his voice swamped her in longing for him. 'Just fine, except that I'm lonely for you. You got home okay?'

'No, I'm still on the motorway.'

She laughed. 'Okay, sorry, silly question.'

'How was the flight?'

'Oh, boring, tiring. Adam . . . I've seen Warren and it's all okay. He understands. I don't have to work notice, so it will just depend how long it takes me to pack up my apartment. I'll have a dealer take my furniture; there's no point in paying the earth to have it shipped. In a few days I'll be on my way home. Really home. It feels good.'

'It sounds good, too,' he assured her. 'Are you sure you're not going to get any argument from Warren?'

'I think he's already used all his best shots. Oh, he knows it would never have worked out between him and me. He was more or less convinced of that even before he saw me. He had a letter from Dad, asking him to do all he could to get me together with you.'

It seemed a long time before Adam said, 'Oh?'

'Yes, I thought it was odd, too. There were one or two things I didn't understand, but we'll talk about that when I get back. I do understand why you couldn't be honest with me.'

Again he let several seconds tick by before he said, 'About what?'

'About his illness. What else was there?'

'Oh—yes,' Adam said sadly. 'I'm sorry, but he was absolutely adamant that we were not to let you know.'

'That's what I thought. I feel terrible about it, but I don't blame you. I know how stubborn Dad could be. But I still should have realised he'd been ill, if I'd had my wits about me. It must have been awful for you and Louise. That's why you moved into Yethfall House, isn't it—because he was ill and you didn't want him to be alone?'

'Partly, yes. I was glad to do what I could. What else did he say in the letter?'

'Oh, he rambled a bit. He probably wasn't thinking too clearly. But he did say you and I were meant for each other. I can't remember exactly what else. I'll show you the letter when I get back.'

'Yes, do that. And make it soon. You seem to be off in some limbo. I can't picture your surroundings. Where are you now?'

She described her apartment and the view from the window. They went on talking, reluctant to end the contact, until Adam

118

reminded her of the cost of transatlantic calls.

'Give me your number,' he suggested, 'and tomorrow I'll phone you to save you running up enormous bills.'

'The bills will be the same, here or there,' she said, amused. 'Yethfall House expenses are down to me now, remember?'

'Even so, I'll reimburse you for calls I make. I hope you're not going to be the kind of wife who insists on handling household finances. I'm a qualified accountant, you know. You can leave that side of things to me.'

Now it was Jenny's turn to hesitate, thrown into a heat of confusion by that word "wife". 'Aren't you getting a little ahead of yourself? We haven't mentioned marriage.'

'We have. At least, I have. Just a moment ago. Didn't you hear me?'

She was too happy to think. Tears bit behind her eyes as she convinced herself that putting him off yet again would be unkind, especially when she was sure of what she wanted.

'Well?' Adam prompted.

'Well . . . okay,' she managed.

'Okay what?'

'Okay . . . darling?'

Adam's husky laugh sent a shiver of sensual pleasure through her. 'I like it, but it wasn't what I meant. I want you to say what it is you're agreeing to undertake.'

She took a deep breath to control herself,

then said through a catch in her throat, 'I'm agreeing to marry you, Adam Carfield. The answer is yes. Yes, yes, yes.'

'Oh, why are you so far away?' he groaned. 'Jenny, my darling girl, come home to me soon. I love you.'

'And I love you,' she replied with contentment and conviction.

*　　　*　　　*

She spoke to Adam on the phone every day, relaying news of her progress. It all took longer than she had anticipated, but at last she was able to book a flight home. On her last night in the States, Warren took her to dinner at the most expensive restaurant in town. There were soft lights, music, wonderful food and wine, but the man was the wrong one and he knew it.

'All you're thinking about is tomorrow,' he said as they lingered over coffee. 'You haven't been with me tonight, you've been winging across the Atlantic to some fellow I've never even seen. Are you sure he's one of the good guys, Jenny?'

'I couldn't be more sure.'

'The fact that you're a rich woman doesn't enter into it, eh?'

She had drunk three glasses of wine and was in the mood to let her irritation show. All evening Warren had kept making remarks like that. 'You're obsessed about that, Warren. I'm not a rich woman, not by your standards.'

'How do you know, if you haven't seen the figures?'

'I just know! My father was comfortably off, but certainly not rolling in it. And anyway it has nothing to do with Adam and me.'

'Money is always a factor in everything.'

'You're so cynical,' Jenny said with disgust. 'Honestly, I'm seeing a side of you I never knew existed. If you really want to know, Adam did his very best to persuade me to sell up and cut off my roots in England, until he was absolutely convinced I'd made up my mind. It was only then that he let himself show what he was feeling. So he didn't manipulate me, whatever you say.'

Warren's calculator brain was working again. She could almost see the electrons whirling behind blue eyes. 'He wanted you to sell up? But that wasn't what your father wanted. Your father had given him the green light. You remember what he said in that letter—"Adam is willing"—Are you telling me that when you got there he did his darnedest to get rid of you?'

She stood up a little unsteadily, holding onto the back of her chair. 'I refuse to listen to any more of this. You're just trying to poison my mind against him because you're jealous. That's not love, Warren, that's dog-in-the-mangerishness.'

Warren got up, taking her arm and glancing around the restaurant as if to see whether they were being observed. 'Go fix your face,' he said. 'I'll see you in the lobby.'

After tonight he would not have to worry about the gossips, Jenny thought. She would be gone and people could make of it what they pleased. She hoped the effects of the wine would put her to sleep so that morning would soon come and she could be away, back to Adam.

In the cab, on the way back to her apartment, Warren said: 'I can't help it, there's something nags me about this whole thing— and don't tell me it's sour grapes or sore pride because I've tried to stay objective. You know me, Jenny. You've always trusted my advice. Well, right now my instincts are yelling foul play. I don't know why, or how, but I won't be happy until you've seen that lawyer and got everything spelled out for you.'

'So I'll do that,' she said. 'Then will you be satisfied?'

'At least I'll know you're not being cheated. You call me the minute you've seen the lawyer. Okay?'

'Okay!' Twitching with annoyance, she was glad to see her apartment building slide into sight. She did not ask Warren in for coffee.

CHAPTER SEVEN

The morning was hectic. She packed her final belongings and waited for the van to collect her trunk, which would be shipped to England. Next came the men from the dealer who had bought the contents of her apartment, and in between there were last-minute visits from friends and neighbours wishing her well. Finally she was all alone in an empty, echoing apartment with her hand luggage and the one suitcase she was taking on the flight. She stood at the window watching the street, wishing she had not agreed to let Warren take her to the airport. Would he try to influence her against Adam again?

Now that the time to leave was almost here, she felt a little apprehensive. Was she really making the right decision? Warren had laid doubts in her mind like snake's eggs and they were incubating in spite of all her efforts to ignore them.

She glanced at the phone which sat on the windowsill. She could call Adam. But he was probably at the office; in England it was mid-afternoon. Then the thought fled, because down in the street she saw a shining grey Rolls Royce Silver Ghost slide up to the kerb and a uniformed chauffeur get out to open the door for Warren.

The chauffeur carried her bags and put them in the trunk before getting behind the wheel, separated from his passengers by a sound-proof glass screen.

'I thought I'd make sure you departed in style,' Warren said as several people waved from the sidewalk. 'I know you have a Rolls of your own now, but—'

'I don't,' she broke in. 'Dad sold it.'

'Sold it?' Warren echoed in disbelief. 'But he was so proud of his Rolls. It was vintage, wasn't it? Didn't he belong to some Rolls Royce club?'

'Yes, but presumably when he was ill he couldn't drive it. The steering was heavy, and it was hopelessly impractical around those narrow lanes. There's a VW Scirocco instead. I much prefer it.'

'Don't you know what he did with the Rolls?'

'I didn't ask! I expect he let it go to some other enthusiast who would appreciate it. Warren, please stop trying to make mysteries where there aren't any. I'd hate us to quarrel at this late stage.'

'Okay.' He reached for her hand, tucking it between his. 'We won't talk about it. You just shut your eyes and hope for the best.'

'My eyes are wide open! Oh . . . you don't know anything about it! You've never even been to Yethfall Dale. You don't know Adam.'

'No, but I met your father. I'm just trying to

do what he asked. I'm looking out for your best interests.'

'Why? Because I'm a stupid child, in your estimation?' She tried to take her hand from his, but he held her fast.

'You're not a child. And you're not stupid. But you do think with your emotions rather than your head. You're impulsive, stubborn, warmhearted, and in many ways you're still an innocent. I've been around longer than you have, Jenny. And I honestly don't think you're in any mental condition to know what's good for you right now.'

'Then you're wrong! I know exactly what I'm doing.'

Warren watched her for a moment, his expression softening. 'Okay, we won't discuss it any more.'

It seemed there was nothing else to talk about. They rode in the back of the luxurious car watching the streets and the morning traffic, her hand still tucked in his. She allowed him that comfort because she owed it to him, and because part of her—a tiny part—was still scared of the finality of the decision she had taken.

At the airport they waited in silence, both of them tense, but when her flight was called she experienced a sense of release. At last she was going home. Home where she belonged. Home to Adam.

'Keep in touch,' Warren pleaded. 'Don't let

me lose you altogether. Hey . . . invite me to the wedding, why don't you? I'd like to meet your Adam Carfield.'

All at once she was choked. She reached to brush a kiss across his cheek. 'Goodbye, Warren. And . . . thanks. Thanks for everything.'

She thought he was going to let it end there, but he suddenly reached out and pulled her close to kiss her full on the mouth with a passionate despair that left her breathless.

'Don't forget I'm here,' he said, his own eyes awash. 'Jenny, I truly hope it all goes the way you want it to go, but . . . Don't do anything rash. Don't marry Carfield until you're sure.'

Then he was gone, shouldering among the crowd as if he couldn't wait to put her behind him.

*   *   *

Warm June darkness had reached England by the time the eastbound plane came in to land. It was near midnight. As she passed through the usual arrivals procedure Jenny saw Adam waiting for her beyond the barrier and soon she was flying into his arms, to hold him with all her might.

'I thought you'd never get here,' he said, studying her face with bright eyes before kissing her in a way that told her how he had missed her. She felt the same. It was marvellous to be home at last.

'Lord, but I've missed you,' he sighed. 'Don't ever go away again.'

'Never,' she vowed.

He lifted his head, his expression suddenly serious. 'Promise me. Whatever happens, you'll never leave me.'

'I promise.' But the look on his face puzzled her. 'What could happen? What do you mean?'

'Oh, I'm superstitious when I get too happy. I never believe it can last. Let's go. The hotel's not far away.'

'Hotel?' Jenny queried.

'I didn't fancy driving through the night,' he replied, and on an afterthought, 'Single rooms, of course.'

'Oh, of course.'

Adam laughed, picked up her case and led the way to the exit.

He drove her to a luxury motel only a few miles from the airport, and Jenny took a welcome shower. She put on a voluminous wrap, fastening it with a tie-belt round her slender waist, and fluffed out her damp hair before going back to the bedroom, where Adam was reclining in one of two chairs by the window. On a low table beside him, a tray with sandwiches and a big pot of coffee waited. Alongside it lay a snapshot of Jenny at eighteen, laughing, with the wind tossing a mane of bright golden hair. She sat down and studied it with a smile.

'I'd forgotten about this,' she said. 'I was desperately young, wasn't I? Is this the picture that Cathy Brent saw?'

'Yes. And I was embarrassed about it so she guessed . . .'

'I'm glad she did. I like her, I hope we can be friends. And, since we're on the subject . . . Are you aware that you came in whistling that Sunday you'd been with her?'

'Oh, you heard me?'

'I was listening for you.'

A slow grin creased his face. 'That's why I came in whistling.'

'Adam Carfield—'

'No, wait!' He held up his hands to fend off any attack. 'I just came across that photo when I was looking for something else I wanted to show you. This.'

'This' was an official-looking document, signed and stamped. Jenny turned hot and cold as she saw that it was a special wedding licence which dispensed with the need to call banns over a three-week period. It meant that she and Adam could be married right away. But the thought only dismayed her.

Seeing her face, he leaned to take hold of her hands. 'Aren't you pleased? Don't you want to be my wife as soon as possible?'

'Adam . . .' She looked from the licence to his face. 'Yes, of course I do, but . . . I thought we'd wait six months at least.'

'What for?'

There didn't seem to be a good answer to that, except, 'It's barely a month since my father died. What would people think?'

'Do we care what people think? We don't have to make a big splash. The vicar will fit us in on Thursday afternoon. Louise—and maybe Tom Hackenthwaite—can stand as witnesses.'

'But you should have asked me!!' she cried, leaping to her feet. 'We've talked on the phone. Why didn't you consult me about this?'

'I thought it would be a nice surprise.' His voice and his face were both expressionless. He had retreated behind that blank mask where she couldn't guess at his thoughts.

'It would have been, at any other time. But not now, Adam. Don't you see, it would be . . . disrespectful. I can't do it.'

'I see.' Something in his face reminded her of the way he had looked six years before, when she had rejected his proposal.

'I only mean for now!' she said desperately. 'In six months' time I'll be only too happy to marry you. Darling—' she threw herself to her knees by his chair—'please try to understand, You loved my father, too. We can't enjoy our wedding so soon after losing him.'

'Even though it was what he wanted?'

Why did she have the feeling she was being rushed? Those snake-eggs that Warren had planted in her mind were hatching and starting to wriggle. 'Don't do anything rash,' he had begged. 'My instincts are yelling foul play.'

'Adam . . . I'm sorry, but I can't. I just can't.'

Adam watched her and must have seen her distress for he reached to take her face between his hands. 'It's all right. It doesn't matter. We love each other. We'll be together. That's the important thing.'

He kissed her hard, then he picked up the special licence and crumpled it in his hand before throwing it across the room.

'That's got rid of that. You're right, anyway. It was a lousy idea. Look, sit down and have some supper. I'm not very hungry myself. I think I'll go and get some sleep. If you'll excuse me.'

The sandwiches tasted like cardboard, though that was because of her mood. She wasn't hungry, and she wasn't sleepy. She sat up into the small hours, wondering if Adam was equally wakeful. How could he ever have entertained the idea of a hasty wedding? Was it because he wanted to be sure of her? Was he afraid she might change her mind and reject him, as she had once before? Or was there something else behind it?

The constraint remained the following morning. Adam was quiet, and distinctly edgy. After an early breakfast they checked out of the hotel and started on the journey home, but instead of happy talk there were long silences between them.

130

'Aren't you ever going to forgive me?' she asked as they sped up the motorway. 'Adam, please! Don't be this way.'

He gave her a brief, quelling glance. 'I have forgiven you. Can we forget about it?'

'We're still going to be at Yethfall House together.'

'I said forget it, Jenny.'

'How can I? I feel as though I've been alone since last night. What are you thinking about?'

'For God's sake! Must you keep on and on? You have to keep picking at the scab to see if it's better yet. For heaven's sake, give it a rest.'

Stricken by the bitterness in his voice, she said, 'I only want you to know I didn't mean to hurt you.'

'I know that. But whether you meant it or not it happened. Yes, I'm upset. I wanted to surprise you. I wanted to sweep you off your feet. But you won't let me. Fine, so you're entitled to your own opinion. I'll get over it, if you'll just give me time.'

'Is that all it is?'

'What else could it be? Look, do you mind keeping quiet so I can concentrate on the road? There are a lot of heavy lorries about. We don't want to drive into the back of one, do we?'

Jenny subsided, though she herself was hurt. She did not understand why he was so uptight. Was there something else on his mind?

By the time they stopped for lunch at a

131

motorway services restaurant Adam was more his old self. He said he was sorry for losing his temper. He supposed he was tired. He had hardly slept for worrying while she was away.

'Worrying about what?' she asked.

'About you, being a thousand miles away with your millionaire. Didn't he even try to get you back?'

'He made a pitch or two. Is that what's eating you? You surely don't think it's because of him that I . . . Adam, what did you do with that special licence? Have you still got it?'

'It's not the sort of thing you leave lying around in hotel bedrooms, is it?'

'Then . . . if it's the only way to convince you I'm not going to run out again . . . if we can do it really quietly . . .'

Oblivious to the other diners, he reached out and took her hand, drawing it to his lips. Over it, his eyes shone with relief. 'Darling! You will? You'll marry me on Thursday?'

'But we'll keep it to ourselves, won't we? You do honestly think that Dad wouldn't mind?'

'He'd have been thrilled. Believe it, Jenny Wren. He'll be there with us, I know. When you marry me it will put everything right. Shall we have some more coffee?'

Seeming glad to prolong his break from driving, Adam fetched some more coffee, saying it ought to be champagne to celebrate their engagement.

'But tell me—about this letter your father wrote to Oxenford.'

'Oh . . . yes, I've been meaning to show you that. Here.' She dug into her bag and brought out the airmail envelope.

While Adam read the letter she watched the traffic race by beyond the glass wall of the motorway restaurant, though she was also watching Adam's reaction. What he read made him grieve afresh. It had done the same to her.

'I read it over and over on the plane,' she said. 'What did he mean about his life being futile?'

'He saw himself as a failure,' Adam replied.

'But why? He made a success of the business.'

'Perhaps he didn't think so. His marriage failed. He was alone.'

'No, he wasn't,' she objected. 'He had you, and Louise. He could have had me there, too, if he'd wanted.'

'Sometimes a man can be surrounded by family and friends and still feel alone.'

Jenny thought about that. 'I suppose we're all alone in our heads. But what do you make of that bit about having so little to give me? And what did he mean by "*If ever she finds out the truth . . .?*" What truth? About his illness?'

'Probably so.' He folded the letter carefully and replaced it in its envelope, regarding her sadly. 'Jen, don't analyse it too closely. He was very sick. He was in despair. Be comforted that

133

his last thoughts were for you—for us. He would be happy to know it had worked out the way he wanted it.'

'I guess so,' she said.

* * *

At Yethfall House they were greeted ecstatically by Gem, and less overpoweringly, if with equal warmth, by Louise. Jenny looked on her kingdom with pleasure and pride. Home at last.

'It's on for Thursday,' Adam told the housekeeper. 'Will you act as witness for us, Louise?'

Louise looked from him to Jenny, her eyes brimming. 'Oh, I'm so happy for you! Your father would have been so pleased! Jenny, my dear . . .' She hugged Jenny, kissing her cheek warmly.

'You don't think it's too soon?' Jenny asked.

'Not in the circumstances, no. I think it's wonderful.'

Jenny didn't know whether to be flattered that Adam hadn't been able to keep the news to himself, or offended because he had told Louise first. She couldn't seem to think for a fog in her head. Her body-clock was disorientated by jet-lag, as she discovered over dinner that night when she was assailed by tiredness and could hardly eat the delicious meal Louise had prepared.

'I could sleep for a week,' she told Adam.

'Then why don't you get to bed? I could do with a good night's rest myself. Get my strength up for Thursday.'

The look in his eyes made her blush. In two days' time she would be Mrs Adam Carfield. Why did she still have the feeling she was being stampeded into it? Adam wanted to be sure of her this time, and who could blame him?

'Okay.' She stifled a yawn and tried to shake herself alert. 'Oh, I'm sorry. It's hit me like a tidal wave. Apologise to Louise for me, will you? I think I'll go straight up.'

She left the table and went to kiss him goodnight. 'See you in the morning, darling. Oh . . . I know what I was going to ask you. Mr Wickham did leave a copy of Dad's will here, didn't he?'

'Yes, it's in the safe in the study.'

'Oh, good. I just want to have a look at it. But it'll do tomorrow. Goodnight, my love.'

She slept a solid fourteen hours, waking to find that Adam had already gone to the office, though he must have been in to see her because she found a note from him on her pillow.

'Dear Sleeping Beauty,' it read. 'I phoned the vicar and confirmed the arrangements for Thursday. You and I have a date for 3pm. Love you. Yours (all of me, always), Florizel.'

She pressed a kiss on the note. 'Darling

135

Adam. Thursday, yes.'

When she had dressed and breakfasted, she went to the study with the idea of reading her father's will—only because Warren had made such a thing of it and she wanted to phone him and tell him how disgraceful his suspicions had been. But the safe was locked, with no key to be found.

She went to ask Louise about it, but Louise shook her head. 'Sorry, I've no idea where it is. Mr Carfield's probably got it.'

'Why would he have the key to my father's safe?'

'Well, for . . .' Louise floundered, her face reddening. 'For safety, I suppose. You wouldn't want somebody just picking it up and looking in the safe, would you?'

'Somebody like whom?'

'Well . . . a burglar.'

Jenny laughed. 'There's nothing in there worth stealing, is there? Well, is there? Don't tell me Dad was hoarding jewels!'

'I've no idea what's in there,' Louise said stiffly. 'How could I? You'll have to ask Mr Carfield.'

'I'll do that,' Jenny said and went straight to the phone to dial the number of Hollander's. The receptionist put her through to Sarah Simmons.

'Oh, Miss Hollander!' the contralto purred, bringing out all Jenny's cat instincts. 'Yes, I'll put you through. By the way, I gather

136

congratulations are in order.'

Jenny caught her breath. 'Where did you hear that?'

'From Mr Carfield. I know one doesn't, as a rule, congratulate the prospective bride, but in this case . . . well, it's quite a coup for you. Mr Carfield must be one of the most eligible bachelors in Derbyshire. You're a lucky girl. Hold on, please, and I'll let you talk to him.'

A moment later Adam came on the line, sounding pleased. 'Jenny! So you're up at last. Feeling better?'

'Fighting fit, thank you. But do mind what you say. There may be piranhas on the line.'

He laughed. 'Sarah knows better than to listen in to private conversations. You've got her all wrong.'

'I doubt that. And just what have you told her? She congratulated me. You promised we'd keep it quiet.'

'All I did was mention to Sarah that you and I would be getting married some day. Perhaps I shouldn't have said that much, but she asked how you were and . . . forgive me, I'm just immensely happy about it. I want the world to know.'

'It's mutual,' she said, her blood responding to that husky note in his voice. 'But I didn't realise, until she told me, that you were "one of the most eligible bachelors in Derbyshire". Don't eligible bachelors have to be filthy rich as well as young and handsome?'

'My rich auntie died and left me a fortune,' Adam said.

'*Now* he tells me,' she laughed. 'But I mustn't keep you from your work. I rang to ask if you've got the key to Dad's safe. I can't find it anywhere and Louise says she knows nothing about it.'

'Yes, I've got it. Not that it would work on its own. You have to know the combination. Why are you so desperate to look at the will?'

'I'm not desperate, exactly, just curious. Isn't it about time I took an intelligent interest?'

'Tell you what, I'll come home for lunch and we'll open the safe together. Warn Louise, will you?'

So there, Warren Oxenford, Jenny thought. Adam isn't trying to keep anything from me. It's all in your nasty suspicious mind.

When Adam came home that lunchtime he opened the safe at once, taking out a long envelope which he handed to Jenny. She read it at the table over a light midday meal, frowning over the phraseology.

As Mr Wickham had said, there were one or two small bequests, notably a sum of five hundred pounds for Louise. And then: 'I devise and bequeath all the residue of my real and personal estate whatsoever and wheresoever not hereby disposed of as to my freeholds in fee simple and as to my personal estate absolutely unto my daughter Jennifer

Anne Hollander for her own absolute use and benefit.'

In essence, the will said exactly what Mr Wickham had told her.

She let out a long sigh of relief as she folded the document and returned it to its envelope.

'Do you think Warren Oxenford will be satisfied now?' Adam asked in a quiet, deliberate tone.

She looked up, startled, knowing her flush betrayed her. 'How—'

'When you come home and immediately want to check up on your rights,' Adam said, 'it's obvious somebody's been putting ideas in your head. Who else but your millionaire?'

Embarrassed, Jenny got out a breathy laugh. 'It's just the way he is. The circle he moves in, nobody trusts anybody. He seemed to think I'd been a bit casual accepting Mr Wickham's word instead of having some third party go through the will with a fine-tooth comb. Well, I've done what he asked—I've checked for myself, and now I'll phone him and tell him he was worrying unduly.'

'Is it really any of his business?'

'He's only doing what Dad asked in that letter.'

'And what, exactly, did he think you might discover?'

'I don't know—except he kept hinting that you were after me for my money.'

Adam's expression was difficult to interpret,

being an odd mixture of wryness and affection. 'That's one thing I can assure you of, Jenny. Your inheritance isn't of the slightest importance to me—not in the way your millionaire thinks.'

'That's what I told him,' Jenny said. 'But he was so adamant that I promised to check just to set his mind at rest.' She laid the long envelope near his place. 'You'd better put this back in the safe. You're the executor.' Leaning her chin on her hands, she surveyed him with adoring eyes, admiring the sweep of dark hair and the beloved lines of his face. 'There's only one thing that bothers me.'

'What's that?'

'That he didn't leave you anything. You were like a son to him, yet apart from being named as executor you're not mentioned in the will. It's strange that he didn't remember you.'

Adam got out of his chair and came to bend over her. 'Tomorrow I shall have the only thing I want.' Responding to the look in his eyes, she reached to meet his mouth and was shaken by the emotion that jolted through her. He lifted her from the chair and held her against him, ravishing her lips and her senses.

Jenny pressed her face into the curve of his throat. 'That's what Dad hoped for. What's mine is yours. We'll share it all, Adam, the way Dad intended.'

His arms tightened painfully as he kissed

her again, confirming all that lay between them before he eased away with a sigh of regret. 'I must get back to work. I'll see you tonight, darling.'

With only a day in which to prepare herself for her wedding, Jenny decided a shopping trip was necessary. She would buy a plain, subdued outfit and perhaps decorate it with a flower or two. Making Gem stay with Louise, so he didn't get under the wheels of the car, she went out along the drive and opened the big gates. As she pushed the second door back, clearing her exit, a car slid up and stopped, right across the gateway, its driver getting out.

About to remonstrate with him, Jenny froze in disbelief.

The arrival was Warren Oxenford.

He was dressed casually in blue slacks and pullover with an open-necked shirt, but there was nothing casual about the way he strode grimly round the car and grasped her arm.

'Get in the car, Jenny.'

She moved two steps and stopped, pulling against the hand that held her captive. 'Warren . . . what on earth are you doing? Where did you spring from?'

'I flew over on the Concorde, if that's what you mean,' he said, his mouth set in determined lines. 'And thank God I did. I've spent the last hour with your Mr Wickham, and what he refused to say told me plenty. That's where we're going—to make him talk.

Get in the car.'

Her mind was spinning. 'How did you know where to find him?'

'You told me his name. It's the kind of thing I remember. I found him easy enough—in the yellow pages under "Solicitors". But he was close-mouthed, even after I showed him my copy of your father's letter and told him I was looking out for you.' Slowly but surely, he was manoeuvring her nearer the car. 'You've got to come with me. It's the only way we'll find out that "truth" your father talked about.'

Jenny felt she was trapped in a nightmare, but this time there was no Adam to wake her and soothe her. There was only Warren, grim and inexorable.

'I've seen the will!' she protested. 'It says just what Mr Wickham told me! Everything my father had, he left to me. I won't go with you and make an utter fool of myself. I've got things to do. I'm getting married tomorrow.'

'You're what?!' Blue eyes blazed with fury. 'I might have known Carfield wouldn't wait. You promised me not to rush into anything.'

'I know I did, but—'

He released her arm and opened the passenger door of his car, standing by it expectantly. 'All right! Make your own choice. If I'm wrong, I'll apologise. But if you don't come with me right now I'll go back home and wash my hands of you. I knew there was something wrong. And now I've seen Wickham

I'm even more convinced. He won't divulge his clients' affairs to an outsider, but not even he could hide what I saw in his eyes. There's something he hasn't told you, as sure as God made little green apples.'

She was frightened now. She had been so happy. She didn't want to spoil it. Yet there had been things that didn't entirely fit—things she had chosen to ignore or gloss over—and she *had* felt that Adam was trying to hustle her into marriage.

'I shall have to go with you,' she said dully. 'You've put doubts in my mind that I can't ignore. But you're wrong, Warren, and I shall never forgive you for frightening me like this. I don't believe Adam would do anything to hurt me.' She stepped nearer to the car, a hand on the edge of the door. 'That is where we're going, isn't it—to Mr Wickham's office? You haven't got some crazy idea about kidnap?'

'Honey,' said Warren with a humourless smile. 'Sure I have, but I'll resist the temptation. We're going to see your family lawyer. Afterwards, if that's what you want, I'll bring you right back home.'

As they drove towards Shadwell he told her how he had brooded over her father's letter and finally taken it to a psychologist to get professional advice.

'He should have told you you were suffering from delusions,' Jenny said bitterly.

'But he didn't.' Warren's level glance said he

wasn't going to be drawn into a war of words. 'Anyhow, I couldn't stop thinking about it so I decided to come over and see for myself. As soon as I mentioned who I was and why I was there I could see Wickham start to sweat. He refused to talk to me unless he had your permission, so I said I'd bring you with me. He'll be waiting for us.'

James Wickham was, indeed, waiting for them in a small office that smelled of dust and old documents. Open shelves on the wall held papers bound in red ribbon and sealed with wax, and on a desk which had seen many years service more papers were strewn in apparent disorder, with among them a pot containing a red geranium.

The solicitor asked them to sit down and himself retreated behind his desk to wipe his half-moon spectacles on a handkerchief. He seemed worried by Warren's demanding presence.

'This is rather irregular,' he said. 'Miss Hollander, wouldn't you prefer that we speak alone?'

'I'm staying,' Warren stated.

'Mr Oxenford is a good friend,' Jenny added, still feeling that she was in a mad dream: obviously Mr Wickham did have things which he would have preferred not to tell her.

'Very well.' The solicitor balanced his spectacles on the end of his nose and looked at her over them with a sigh of resignation. 'What is it you want to know?'

'We want to know exactly what's coming to Jenny under the terms of her father's will,' Warren said.

'Exactly? Why . . . I'm not sure myself yet. These things take time. To evaluate the estate will mean taking an inventory of everything. His clothes, his books, his personal possessions . . .'

'Don't give us the run-around,' Warren said. 'Try a guesstimate. How much are Hollander shares worth on today's market?'

'Really . . . I've no idea. I'm not a broker.'

'Then what about the house?'

Mr Wickham surveyed him with as much expression as a waxwork's figure, and Jenny felt as though everything had stopped—her heart, her breath, even time itself. Eventually he turned his mild blue eyes in her direction.

'Mr Wickham . . .' she managed. 'The house?'

'The house . . . is not part of your father's estate.' The words seemed to be dragged out of him. 'I'm very sorry, Miss Hollander. You will have his personal possessions, his car and so forth, and whatever money is left after the other bequests have been settled, though I fear it will not amount to much. Your father also retained a thirty per cent interest in Hollander Craft Furnishings Ltd, which will also come to you.'

'He sold the house?' she breathed in total

disbelief.

'*And* his majority holdings in the business, from the looks of it,' Warren added in disgust. 'No wonder they didn't want you to know. So who owns the house now, Mr Wickham? Who owns the business?'

Mr Wickham looked at Jenny with a sympathy that terrified her. 'The house, and the majority holding of shares in Hollander's, belong to Mr Adam Carfield.'

Jenny felt turned to stone. It was too incredible for her to take in. Her mind seemed to have been wiped clean of thought.

Warren leapt to his feet. 'Hell's teeth! That guy just bided his time and then took a defenceless old man for everything he had.' He swung round to look at Jenny. 'This is the man you're going to marry? My God, the guy's a stinking, thieving rat!'

CHAPTER EIGHT

Jenny stared at an expanse of water that rippled in the wind, reflecting a sky where bright cumulus clouds hung almost motionless. She was aware of the peace of the place, disturbed only by the wind moving in the pines and by the odd bleat from one of the wandering sheep, but it seemed to exist in a different world from where she was.

She and Warren had driven out of Shadwell to the track which ran beside the reservoir, where pines grew on steep hillsides above a drowned valley. She supposed she must have directed him, for he would never have found it by himself. She had not been here many times. Maybe once or twice before, years ago—with Adam.

Bracken and twigs cracked behind her and Warren came back from his walk to stand beside her on the hill. 'How much longer are you going to sit there? We've got to talk.'

'About what?'

'About what you're going to do now! You can't stay here, Jenny. Come back to the States with me. I'll put my lawyers onto this. Carfield won't get away with it.'

Jenny spread her hands in front of her, palms upwards. They were trembling. 'I can't believe he would do such a thing. Not Adam.'

'You heard what Wickham said. Would he lie to you? Your father was alone, a sick old man. Carfield moved in and took him for all he could get. Now he wants the rest—and you along with it.'

'But Adam's not like that!' she said wretchedly.

'Don't be a fool, Jenny. What other explanation is there? He sucked your father dry.'

'It's funny,' she said, staring at her hands. 'Only this lunchtime I was saying how odd it was that Dad hadn't mentioned him in his will. He didn't need to, did he? Adam already had most of it.' She buried her face in her hands as her mind started to work again. 'Oh, I should have known! He was obviously in total control at Hollander's. And Louise took orders from him. Every time I talked about the house being mine she got flustered. *And* when I asked her why he had the key to the safe. They were in league, the two of them, to keep me from knowing . . . It's all so obvious now. And yet they both pretended to be so fond of Dad! How could they?'

'You trusted them. They relied on that—and on the fact that you were upset. You helped them pull the wool over your own eyes.'

It was true, she thought in despair. She *had* trusted Adam and Louise, had closed her eyes to words and events which ought to have made

148

her suspicious. She didn't believe the facts even now, yet they must be true—Adam had taken control of the business, and possession of the house, from an old man who trusted him and who had no one of his own around to protect him.

'At least this explains why he tried to get you to go away—so he could cover it all up until it was too late for you to do anything about it,' Warren said.

'Then why did he ask me to marry him?'

'That was after you decided to stay. A wife can't testify against her husband, can she?'

She looked up, blinking sore eyes in the wind. 'That's ludicrous! He hasn't done anything criminal.'

'How do you know?'

'I just know! Oh, none of it makes sense! Adam loved my father. He'd never plot to rob him of everything. Unless . . .' She stared unseeingly at the lake as a new theory sent chills through her.

'Well?' Warren demanded. 'Unless what?'

'Unless it was me he was trying to hurt. He had good reason to hate me. But perhaps . . . perhaps he changed his mind, after I came home. Perhaps he was sorry for it, and trying to make it up to me. He did say . . .'

'He said what?'

'That marrying me would make everything all right. He made me promise not to leave him, whatever happened.'

What a fool she had been to put so much trust in Adam. Even if he was sorry now—even if he genuinely loved her—things could never be the same because he was not the man she had believed him to be.

From close beside her, Warren said: 'Let me take you home, hon'. Come back to the States with me. Remember your father asked me to look out for you.'

She moved away and got unsteadily to her feet. 'He also wanted me to marry Adam. If Adam had cheated him, he wouldn't have said . . .' She flung her hands to her pounding head. 'It still doesn't make sense! I must see Adam. I've got to hear what he says about it all.'

'He'll have some story cooked up. You'll be safer not to risk getting taken in again.'

'I shan't,' she said, shaking her head. 'You'll be with me, won't you? But he's not a liar, Warren. I can't believe it.'

He threw out his hands. 'How can you say that? If he's not a liar, then how come he didn't happen to mention that he has title to most of your father's property?'

'I don't know! But I'm not going anywhere until I find out.'

She had lost track of the time and was surprised to find it was nearly six as they approached Yethfall House. Adam would be home from the office. Since he had closed the gates, she asked Warren to leave his car outside and together they walked up the drive and the steps.

In the hall, Gem came bounding to meet her and his barking drew an anxious Adam from the sitting-room, saying, 'Jenny, where on earth have—' He stopped as he saw her pale face and reddened eyes, and the silver-haired man who stood beside her glowering. 'What's wrong?' he asked, swiftly stepping towards her. 'Darling, you look—'

'Don't touch her!' Warren snapped, placing himself between them.

The bewilderment on Adam's face made Jenny hurt. 'Don't touch her?' he repeated. 'Why not? Who the hell are you to tell me—'

'It's Warren,' Jenny said hopelessly. 'This is Warren Oxenford.'

'Oh, really?' Adam stepped back to look the older, shorter man up and down. 'Well, I won't say I'm pleased to meet you, Mr Oxenford, especially without the courtesy of any warning. Do you mind if I ask what you're doing here? Are you aware that Jenny and I are getting married tomorrow?'

'I think you'll find those plans are cancelled,' Warren said.

Adam's face became a cold mask. 'Indeed?' He looked at Jenny with eyes like flint. 'Do I warrant an explanation?'

'We've been to see Mr Wickham,' she said with a helpless shrug.

She didn't have to say more; the expression on his face was answer enough. For a moment he stood utterly still; then he let out a long sigh, which seemed to drain all the fight out of him. 'I see.'

'Huh!' Warren snorted. 'He's not even going to bother denying it. You miserable, thieving bastard! You took advantage of a sick old man who trusted you!'

Adam stiffened, his hands clenching and unclenching at his sides; then he looked at Jenny again. 'Is that what you believe?'

'I don't know what I believe,' she said wretchedly. 'Is it true, Adam? Does Yethfall House belong to you? And most of Hollander's?'

His face was unreadable again. 'Yes, it's true.'

'Of course it's true!' Warren exclaimed. 'Go pack a bag, Jenny. I'll take you home.'

But she was watching Adam, wishing she could guess what was going through his mind. 'Why didn't you tell me?'

'I intended to. Some day. I wanted . . . Oh, hell, what does it matter? Whatever I say, you're not going to believe me, not with this . . . this minder between us to fling dirt at me.'

'You want her all to yourself?' Warren asked with an incredulous laugh. 'So you can fill her head with more of your sweet-talking lies? No way, Carfield! No way!'

'I never lied to you,' Adam told Jenny, and now she saw the pain in his eyes. 'No, that's not true—I lied that day in the office, when

152

you asked me why I came looking for you. I did want to stop you from talking to anyone, in case you found out too much too soon. And I suppose I lied when I told you I'd forgotten that summer six years ago. But the rest was true. All of it.'

Including the fact that he loved her: she could see that.

'Do you expect us to believe that?' Warren demanded.

'I don't give a damn what you believe, Oxenford!' Adam snarled. 'I'm talking to Jenny. What the hell gives you the right to come here interfering?'

Jenny's father gave me the right!'

'*Carte blanche* to stick your nose in where it's not wanted—is that the way you read it? You may have forgotten, but it was *me* he intended her for.'

'He was sick. He didn't know what he was saying.'

'He was sick in his body, not in his mind.'

'And how do we know you didn't influence him?'

'Oh, please!' Jenny threw her hands over her ears. 'Listen to yourselves! I am not a bone to be fought over! I'll make up my own mind.'

Giving her a furious glance, Warren subsided.

Jenny turned to Adam. 'Well?'

'What is it you want me to say? I own the house. I own most of the business. You know that now.'

'But how did it come about? Dad would never have sold Yethfall House if he'd known what he was doing. And where would you have got the money? You must have . . . coerced him, in some way. Adam, just tell me. Whatever made you do it, I'll try to understand. Were you punishing me for rejecting you? Is that why you did it? And then, when I came home, did you regret it and try to make up for it?'

Bitter lines played round his mouth. 'If that's what you want to think.'

'Why won't you *tell* me?'

'Because you wouldn't like the truth if you heard it. It doesn't matter now. I was crazy ever to think it might work. Go back to the States, Jenny. Go back and marry Mr Oxenford. He'll take care of you.'

She clenched her fists, wanting to beat him. 'I don't need anybody to take care of me! I'm sick of being treated like a little girl who has to be sheltered from everything. Dad did it, and both of you keep doing it. Why won't you allow me to think for myself? Just tell me what's been going on.'

In the silence she heard the peaceful ticking of the long-case clock in the corner. It seemed to underline the tension that filled the hall.

'I can't,' Adam said at length.

A triumphant, sneering laugh broke from Warren. 'He pleads the fifth amendment!

154

Leave him to stew, Jenny.' He took her arm, drawing her towards the stairs. 'Go pack your bag. We're leaving.'

Her eyes were fixed on Adam's face and she saw there an agony that matched her own. 'Adam, please!'

'No, I can't,' he said, his shoulders slumping. 'You'd better do as your friend says. Go with him. There's nothing left for us now.'

Tears pricked at her eyes. 'Do you really mean that?'

For answer, Adam turned away.

'Oh, tell her the truth!' A distraught Louise rushed from the kitchen doorway where she must have been listening. Her face was wet with tears and so was the apron she twisted in her hands as she stood between them, looking from one to the other. 'Tell her the truth, Mr Carfield. You can't let her go away. This is her home. She belongs here with you. Henry never wanted it to end like this. For his sake, I beg you to tell her the truth.'

He stood unmoving, his back turned, his hands deep in his pockets, stubbornly silent.

'Then I shall!' Louise cried. 'You may have promised, but *I* didn't. Jenny . . .

'Louise, no!' Adam exclaimed, spinning round.

She whirled on him. 'So what shall we do— let her go away believing the worst of you when it was you that saved her father from bankruptcy? When it was you who stepped in

155

and allowed him to die in peace, and with dignity? She's right—she's a grown woman. She has a right to know the truth about her own father, however ugly.'

Jenny found she was holding the banister tightly, poised on the first stair with all her senses straining.

'What truth?' she breathed. 'Louise, *what truth*!'

The housekeeper turned drowned eyes on her. 'Your father . . . your father was deep in debt, Jenny. He was in danger of losing everything. Through gambling.'

A shell-shocked Jenny managed a shaky laugh. 'Oh, you surely don't expect me to believe—'

'You asked for the truth,' Louise broke in. 'This is it. He gambled away everything he had. It was just the horses at first—he liked a little flutter—but then he lost a lot of money when some shares he had failed, and he was afraid he'd have nothing to leave you, so he tried to get it back. Even when he was ill, he was always on the phone to his bookmakers.'

'Are you talking about my father?! This is crazy. He wouldn't . . .' But a glance at Adam's taut face only confirmed that this incredible story was the truth.

Unable to stand any longer, Jenny sat down heavily on the stairs. 'Why didn't somebody stop him?'

'Because we didn't know,' Louise croaked.

'Not until it was too late. About a year ago, he decided to semi-retire. He said he was feeling tired. He sold the Rolls—to make some money to pay his debts, as we found out later, but it wasn't enough. Eventually, he told Mr Carfield the truth. He'd raised a second mortgage on the house to stave off the debt-collectors, but he still owed a lot of money. He was desperate. He knew by then how sick he was and he didn't want to leave you with debts to pay. So as not to let everything go into the hands of strangers, he asked Mr Carfield to buy the house and take more shares in the business, so he could pay off his creditors.'

She glanced at Adam, adding, 'I don't know how much it was and I don't suppose he'll ever tell you. It settled your father's mind, but he didn't want you finding out what a mess he'd made of everything. He hoped you'd never find out, so he made Mr Carfield promise—'

'Louise . . .' Adam said in a low voice full of pain.

'I heard you!' she said. 'I was in the room that last night before he died. You promised to shield Jenny from the truth for as long as you could. And you've tried. You'd even give her up sooner than have her know. But Henry wouldn't have wanted that. He wanted the two of you to be here together, and your children. I know, because he used to talk to me. We were very close those last few months. He told me everything. Jenny . . . is there anything else you want to know?'

Jenny shook her head. 'I think I've heard plenty for now.' She dragged herself upright, glancing briefly at the three people below. 'If nobody minds, I'd like to be alone for a while.'

*   *   *

She sat in her window-seat looking down the green dale where long shafts of evening sunlight streamed. Now, more than ever, she wished she had come home sooner. Perhaps she could have prevented some of the disaster, though if Adam and Louise hadn't realised what was happening, how could she have discovered it on brief visits?

'Your tea,' said Louise, coming in with a tray, her eyes puffy but dry now. 'Jenny, I can't tell you how sorry I was to have to tell you all that, but you had to know.'

'I'm grateful, Louise. You did the right thing.'

'I only hope Mr Carfield thinks so. I can't often tell what he's thinking.'

'Nor can I,' Jenny said ruefully. 'What are they doing now?'

'Talking. Not quarrelling or anything, just talking. I took them some tea, too.'

The thought of Warren sipping tea and making polite conversation with Adam raised a wry smile on Jenny's face. 'All of us have got plenty to think about. Dad must have been

158

terribly unhappy. Not only ill, but sick of himself for what he was doing.'

'Yes, he was. Ashamed. But not able to stop himself. Gambling can get you like that—one more try and you might win back all you lost, but you rarely do, and so it gets worse.'

'So I've heard. But I never imagined Dad . . . For all the letters he wrote to me, he never hinted at what he was going through. Or Adam. It must have been hell for him, too.'

'It was. You . . . You will be staying, won't you?'

Jenny turned away to stare at the view, saying sadly, 'I don't know. Adam promised Dad he'd take care of me, but what were his motives? I don't want his pity.'

'He doesn't pity you. He loves you. If you don't know that—'

'I don't think either of us has been any too clear about feelings and motivations this last few weeks. I can't predict what will happen, Louise. I'm almost too tired to think.'

Louise left her. Jenny was drinking a second cup of tea when someone tapped on her door and Warren's voice said, 'It's me, Jenny. May I come in?' He closed the door behind him and stood by it with his head on one side. 'Well?'

'Don't ask me. I don't know. I don't intend making any more snap decisions this side of my ninetieth birthday.'

'A changed woman?' His smile held affection and despondency. 'Don't change too

159

much. I came to say that I'm leaving—for now. I guess you and Carfield have a lot to talk over. I'll be at the Granton Arms in Shadwell, if you need me.'

'Thank you, Warren.'

A gesture negated her gratitude. 'I get the feeling I did more harm than good. I should have let well enough alone, but . . .' He sighed heavily, 'I thought I was helping. If you're interested, he seems glad to have everything out in the open.'

'Playing peacemaker, Warren?' Jenny enquired wearily. 'Has he convinced you lie's one of the good guys?'

'Which you told me all along,' he recalled. 'Okay, I should have met the man before I sat in judgement. I told you I'd eat crow if I was wrong, so . . . I apologise. Maybe the world isn't full of rotten apples after all. You'll be okay? Will you call me in the morning?'

'To let you know I've survived the night? Yes, I'll do that.'

Warren left.

Eventually Louise arrived to fetch the tea-tray and ask, 'Do you want any dinner? Mr Carfield's getting ready to take the dog out. Aren't you going down to talk to him? That's what he's waiting for.'

'I don't know what to say.'

'You'll think of something. So what about dinner? Mr Carfield said he'll probably settle for sandwiches later, but I can soon whip up a meal if you're hungry.'

'Sandwiches will be fine for me, too—if I feel like eating at all. Don't worry, Louise. If I want something I can get it myself.'

Louise shook her head. 'Don't worry, she says. Maybe it's none of my business, but I do worry about the two of you. You're both sitting around like lost souls—separately, when you could be together. Won't you go down and see him? He won't come to you. He's too proud.'

Pride? Jenny thought. Was that what it was with her, too?

No, with her it was guilt. She had thought some terrible things about Adam—had said them, too. She couldn't expect him to forgive her. Besides, if she stayed she would always wonder what his real feelings were; she would never know if he loved her or if he was keeping yet another promise made to her father. She couldn't bear to live with a man who only felt sorry for her.

After a while, she saw Adam go out with Gem, heading down the dale as he usually did. He didn't even glance up at her room.

Jenny made up her mind: she would leave before he came back. She would spend the night at a hotel, and in the morning she would decide where she was going. Not with Warren, though. That part of her life was over. She had to pick up the pieces of what was left and start again—on her own feet this time.

She began to pack, slowly and carefully, part

of her hoping that someone would come and stop her. But no one came. Eventually, as the long June day faded, she snapped the last catch, fastened the final buckle. She was ready to leave Yethfall House for what might be the last time.

But she couldn't do it. She couldn't just walk out and not even talk to Adam one last time. He had done so much, both for her and for her father. The least she could do was tell him how grateful she was.

Now that she had made up her mind to see him, she couldn't bear to sit waiting. She would go and meet him.

The sky remained a duck-egg blue with streaks of pink in the west, but in the dale the sun had gone. A shoulder of land hid the lower dale, but soon she was climbing its flank, on steps formed by outcrops of rock worn smooth and slippery over the years. The rocks overhung a deep stretch of the trout stream, with trees growing out from a sheer drop of fifteen or twenty feet, but from the top Jenny could see down into the dale. Below, to the right, the stream rushed over a series of low weirs, ending at a bridge half hidden by bushes, and it was there that she saw a lonely figure accompanied by a dog.

'Adam!' she said almost to herself, but as she started towards him, a swallow swooped right in front of her. She jerked away and her feet slipped on shiny rock. She hit the hillside, hands clawing at short grass. The drop yawned and she slid over it. Branches tore at her skin and clothes. Then her hands fastened round one of the trees and she hung there suspended over a rush of darkening water.

'Adam!' This time it was a yell at the top of her voice, though she doubted he could hear her. She scrabbled with her feet, finding a hold on bouncing branches, but not enough for her to dare release a handhold. 'Oh . . . you stupid idiot!' she moaned at herself. There wasn't much of a drop, and she could swim, but she didn't relish getting soaked while fully dressed.

What seemed like ages later, she heard a dog barking, coming rapidly nearer. Gem appeared silhouetted against the pale sky, paws splayed as he threw back his head to bark more urgently.

She heard Adam's voice, calling her name. Suddenly he was there, his tall figure dark on a background of pink streaks against blue. He threw himself down near the lip of the drop and extended his arm towards her. 'Catch hold of my hand.'

Summoning all her nerve, she let go with one hand, swinging sickeningly from the other in the moment before strong fingers clamped round her wrist. He hauled her up to safety and she sat getting her breath, aware of him on one knee not far away.

'And you reckon you don't need looking after?' he said at length. 'You're not fit to be let out alone, Jenny Hollander. How many times have I warned you about this stretch of rock? Look at you—you're all scratched. Your blouse is torn, and . . . You're bleeding!'

His fingers touched her flesh through a rent in her blouse at one shoulder, and Jenny shrugged away, springing to her feet with a force that unsteadied her and threatened to make her fall again until he leapt up and caught hold of her.

'Here, let's get back to level ground,' he said, taking her hand. 'Unless you really want to go for a twilight swim.'

'There's no need to sound so damn superior!' she snapped, though she went with him to where the meadow opened out and Yethfall House beckoned from behind its walls. 'I forgot where I was standing. I was trying to attract your attention.'

After a moment's silence, he said quietly, 'You've had my full attention since the moment we met.'

Now at last she looked at him, sidelong from under her lashes and a tumbled sweep of golden hair. 'I can't imagine why.'

'No, neither can I. You're a wilful, bad-tempered little brat. And I love you very much.'

She watched him, her thoughts erratic, her heart unsteady. She didn't know what to say.

'What do I have to do to convince you?' Adam asked. 'I've played all my cards. You

164

said you wanted to be allowed to think for yourself. Well, here's your chance. You know how *I* feel. How do *you* feel?'

'Lost,' she said hoarsely. 'There's so much I don't understand.'

'Such as?'

'Oh—everything. Everything! Adam, why didn't you *tell* me?'

'Because your father asked me not to. Wait—' as she started to object. 'That was where it started. Of course I knew I couldn't keep it from you for ever. I originally planned to tell you after the funeral. But then you were injured, so I decided to leave it until you felt better. And your being engaged made a difference. I thought if I could delay until you were safely back with Warren then *he* might help me break the news and it wouldn't be so difficult for you.'

'Except that I decided not to go back,' Jenny said.

Adam blew out an eloquent breath. 'Quite—that change of plan did put a spanner in the works. By then it was a bit late to come straight out with the truth, and anyway I had begun to hope that you and I . . . that we . . .

'And we did.'

'Yes.' He stared at her in the fading light. 'I know this will sound ridiculous, but I had the idea that if I could prevent you from finding out the truth until we were married then somehow, by some miracle, everything would be all right. If you were my wife—if you knew I loved you, and if you trusted me—then you'd understand. Only . . . well, it all went wrong, didn't it?'

'And how!' Jenny sighed.

'If you're wondering where I got the money,' he added, 'I did try to tell you this morning. Five years ago an aunt—a great-aunt I didn't know I had—left me her rambling old house, on a few acres of prime property that some developers were anxious to get hold of. House prices were going through the roof. They paid me a small fortune.'

'And you used it to pay off my father's debts,' she said sadly.

Taking her by the shoulders he pulled her closer, his fingers softly kneading her flesh. 'I used it to invest in property and shares. As it happened, I had the means to do something for a man who had treated me like a son. Please don't deny me the pleasure of knowing I was of some help to him. I didn't lose by it— we didn't lose by it. Hollander's is pretty sound, you know. We'll build it up between us. And we have the house as an added asset.'

'We?' she whispered in anguish. 'Oh, Adam, you can't mean that. After everything I've done? I thought some awful things. I promised I'd never leave you, whatever happened, but I did leave you—oh, not physically, but in my head I deserted you, I doubted you. And now . . .' she spread her hands helplessly. 'I don't

166

know how to thank you, or make it up to you.'

'Keep your promise. Stay with me. Share with me what belongs to us both. I love you. I've always loved you. Nothing is ever going to change that.'

A whirl of emotions swept through her as she watched him and knew, finally, that he meant every word.

'But there's no rush,' he said. 'I'll cancel the arrangements for tomorrow. You were right, we should wait a while. We'll know when the right moment comes. I want you to be sure, Jenny. Very sure.'

She let out a long slow breath. 'I *am* sure. But I'd be grateful for some time. To think, to grieve, to get my head together.'

'All the time you need. No hurry. We have the rest of our lives.'

A shudder of sheer joy ran through her as she lifted her face and surged up to find his mouth. They stood clasped together, lost in each other, while the twilight deepened and the lights of Yethfall House gleamed out across the dale.

We hope you have enjoyed this Large Print book. Other Chivers Press or Thorndike Press Large Print books are available at your library or directly from the publishers.

For more information about current and forthcoming titles, please call or write, without obligation, to:

Chivers Press Limited
Windsor Bridge Road
Bath BA2 3AX
England
Tel. (01225) 335336

OR

Thorndike Press
295 Kennedy Memorial Drive
Waterville
Maine 04901
USA

All our Large Print titles are designed for easy reading, and all our books are made to last.